Witch, Please

By: L.J. Burkhart and

Mandy Maree

contents

To all the magical bitches.
Stay bitchy.
Stay magical.

PROLOGUE

1693

A man dressed in all black stood in the crowd and watched as a pyre was built for the witch he no longer cared for. The witch who he sacrificed in the name of love. She stood there watching her own impending demise as the guards held her. The man's full lips remained still as tears tracked down her cheeks and the sun set in the background. Any other day it would've been idyllic, but considering the sky was about to be filled with smoke, it was quite the opposite. Her green eyes locked with his, a mixture of anger, desire, and fear coating her features. He broke her stare.

She shouted his name, pleading with him. He knew she wanted him to save her.

The crowd buzzed with anticipation. When the pyre was finished, they dragged the witch up by her auburn hair and tied her to the stake as she shrieked in pain and outrage. Despite her screams, he observed the resignation in her eyes and the defeated slump of her posture.

"Burn the witch!" a woman yelled in the crowd.

"Go back to hell where you belong!" another man roared.

As the atmosphere became more violent and charged, he tore his green eyes away from the pyre and scanned the crowd before settling on a familiar face. Her beautiful face. He paused to watch a single tear fall from her dove gray eyes before resting upon her soft, freckled cheek. She wiped it away before anyone else noticed.

She walked away as they brought the torches up to light the pyre, her honey-blond hair swept back in the breeze, and he knew that she didn't want to witness what was about to happen. He didn't blame her.

He hurriedly walked away from the hateful people behind him and the life that was about to turn to ashes in the wind.

He called out her name after they walked a few blocks and were far enough away that they wouldn't hear the screaming that would surely start at any moment.

She stopped but didn't turn toward him.

He called it again. "I know you can hear me."

He heard her sigh before she reluctantly swiveled to face him.

"What do *you* want?" she whispered disdainfully.

"Do you see now why I did what I did?"

"No. I will *never* forgive you for what you did."

"That could've been *you.*"

"It *should've* been me!" Her voice rose to a shout before she broke down into sobs, her hands cradling her face.

He wrapped his arms around her so that her head and hands were resting against his chest. She seemed too lost in her own grief to notice, but after a few seconds, she stiffened and pulled away from him. He thought his heart had already been shattered beyond any further destruction. He was wrong.

"Leave me alone," she said before turning and walking away from him, taking the last of his humanity with her.

His grief and rage combined into a potent mixture that overwhelmed him. "What happened to that witch is *your* fault. You realize that, don't you? And you're right, it *should've* been you."

one

Zara

I park in front of Chad's apartment, excited to finally see him after his business trip. He's been gone for only a week, but today's his birthday, so I want to surprise him. My phone vibrates, and I check to see if it's him, but it's just a text from my sister, Luna.

> Hey Z, I'm home from work already. Have lots of fun with Chad tonight xx

Smiling, I take a quick selfie in the car and send it to her. Before I exit my texts, I click on my message thread with Chad to see if there's anything new from him. Nope. Not since last night when he said "Thanks, cupcake" in response to my text wishing him a "Happy Birthday" at midnight. He's got to be home now though. I checked his flight's status, and it arrived almost four hours ago. I blow out a deep breath before glancing up at his bedroom window on the third floor. The light is on, so maybe he's just been busy unpacking.

I open the car door carefully, trying not to expose the new lingerie set underneath my long jacket. Excitement tingles through my body.

I make my way to his front door and pause for a moment. Something doesn't feel right. My stomach sinks with dread. *Must just be nerves*, I convince myself before brushing it off.

I knock and adjust my jacket, gripping a side in each hand, ready to show him his present.

As the door flings open, so does my jacket, revealing the rose and black lace corset. "Happy Birth—"

"Aww, I think you have the wrong place, sweetie." My eyes widen at an unfamiliar redhead wearing a familiar-looking robe.

I frantically try to cover myself but the jacket falls. "Oh, Maiden, Mother, and Crone, I'm so sorry. This is so embarrassing," I say while picking up my peacoat from the ground and trying not to rip my stockings. In my panic and confusion, I tell myself that I must've gotten turned around and went to the wrong condo. "I thought this was Chad's pl—"

"Who's at the door, cupcake?"

My jaw drops at the voice I know so well. My heart falls to my gut as my cheeks redden with anger.

"It's your *other* cupcake, honey bear," I shout.

"Shit, Zara," he says, approaching the doorway with a towel wrapped around his waist.

The redhead looks from me to him. "I thought you took care of this..."

Excuse me? My blood boils more than any of Luna's potions ever have.

"I thought I did."

"Are you serious, Chad?" I ask, somehow ignoring the fact that there's a skinny half-naked bitch still standing in front of me. Wearing *my* spare robe, I might add.

He pauses and his eyes shift toward the other girl. He clears his throat. "Why don't you go back to bed and wait for me, cupcake?"

I watch in awe as she rolls her eyes and scoffs. "I'm not happy you didn't handle this when you told me you would, but since it's your birthday, I'll let it slide. But make it quick so I can give you your present," she replies, winking before turning around to do as he says. The exchange makes me want to hurl.

I glare at Chad. "How could you?" I whisper.

He brushes his fingers through his hair before setting his hand on his hip. "I can't believe it took you this long to figure it out, *cupcake*."

"This long? How long?"

He shrugs. "A while, I guess."

"And what is a while?" I huff. I really thought he was one of the good guys. I feel like I'm a magnet for terrible men.

"Wait. Remind me, how long have we been seeing each other?"

I flip my dark, long hair over my shoulder. "Screw you, Chad. I thought we were great together." I start to turn away but stop to ask, "Were you even on a business trip?"

"You're making this out to be such a big deal. And I thought you'd be smart enough to realize a mechanic doesn't go on business trips."

"But you told me you were looking to expand your shop." I scoff. "You know what? It doesn't matter." I fight back the tears building up behind my eyes, refusing to let him have the satisfaction. "Have a nice life, *Chad*."

"Already do," he mumbles before slamming the door.

I walk in the front door to our home. Luna is on the couch, sipping wine and watching another episode of *Game of Thrones*. When she glances up at me, she grabs the remote and pauses it. "Sorry, I know this show is a bit too dark for you." She taps her phone to see the time. "Wait, what are you doing here? I thought you were giving Chad his special birthday present now that he's home?"

I finally allow myself to burst into tears. My sister tosses the remote back on the couch and sets her wine down. She rushes over, wrapping her arms around me before giving me the tightest squeeze.

She lets me cry into her arms for a few moments before pulling back.

"What the hell happened?"

I wipe my cheeks to clear some of the moisture, but it just keeps coming. I look down, remembering what I'm wearing. "Wait, shit. I need to change first."

Luna nods her head. "Oh, right. You go change, I'll grab the wine. I got two new bottles of cab from work today."

"I love that you work at a wine bar," I say, referring to Full Bodied. It enables her to constantly bring home fantastic wine for us at the cheapest possible price.

I make my way into my room, stripping off the lingerie as quickly as possible. I open my color-coded pajama drawer. For the first time in my life, I'm overcome with the urge to toss everything and just live carefree like Luna does. The thought quickly dissipates as the rational part of my brain reminds me that I'll be the one to clean it up. Instead, I grab my comfiest set of jammies and put them on. As I'm about to leave my room, I notice the lingerie still on the floor by my bed and decide to leave it there as my own form of protest. *That counts, right?*

I head into the bathroom and take a look at myself in the mirror. Streaks of my black mascara and eyeliner serve as tattoos across my cheeks.

I turn on the faucet before splashing cool water across them. As I use makeup remover to wipe away the remaining stains, Luna walks in with our wine. With the two of us next to each other in the mirror, our differences are striking. My dark brown hair to her almost white blond. The shapes of our noses, mine upturned versus her long, straight one. Finally, our features—mine soft and warm, hers sharp and harsh. The only similarity we share is our dove gray eyes, which we inherited from our grandmother.

"I thought you could use this sooner rather than later," she says as she hands me the wineglass. "I turned on a special movie for you."

I hear the sound of *Hocus Pocus* streaming from the living room and a smile tries to make its way onto my face. Luna knows it's my comfort movie.

"Aww, I wish I had a Binx of my own," I remark when I see his cute face on the screen as we make our way to the couch, the movie already at the part where the witches change him.

"Bitch, focus and spill the tea. I'm dying to know what happened, and I don't give a shit about cats right now," she says.

I roll my eyes at her but tell her everything and she listens intently, a quiet rage building on her face. I inwardly smile at her fierce protectiveness of me. By the time I've finished telling her what happened, we've both finished with our glasses of wine, and she pours us another.

"I have a brilliant beyond brilliant idea," Luna says as she gets up from the couch. I recognize that scheming look in her eyes, and it overrides the humor of her *Parent Trap* quote.

"No," I say. I know that look means she's up to no good.

She ignores me and heads into our Potion Pantry. I sigh, knowing that I can't stop her.

Luna reemerges, spell book in hand.

"Here we go," I mutter under my breath.

She continues ignoring me and opens it to a section I've never dared to look at before. Hexes.

"This fucker is going to get what's coming to him, and we're going to ensure that he does."

"No. I just want to leave this behind. We don't always have to get revenge, Luna."

"He doesn't deserve to get off scot-free. Men like him are too common, and most of the time women can't do anything about it. *We can.* And he didn't just hurt anyone, he hurt *you.* I won't stand by and let him do this to you without any sort of repercussion."

I sigh, knowing my sister and realizing that she will not be deterred. Maybe at this point I can minimize the damage.

"Fine." I look at the spell book, intent on finding something simple. "How about we give him dandruff?"

She scoffs. "No way. Too easy, not to mention that asshole probably already has it with all the hair gel he uses on a daily basis."

I chuckle despite myself.

She flips through the book. "Oooh. A flesh-eating virus."

"Wayyyy too much."

We keep flipping. "Erectile dysfunction?"

"Hmm. Something not as permanent."

"STD?"

"Okay, but nothing too severe. He needs to be able to get it treated." At least I know he hates going to the doctor. That's also tame enough to be my own form of revenge.

"Chlamydia?"

I look it up online just to see how bad it will be. Looks like it can be treated with antibiotics. *Perfect. Clam it is.*

"Done."

Luna smiles in malicious delight, and we make our way to the Potion Pantry, Luna still carrying the book.

"Tell me what we need," I sigh in resignation.

"Oil of boil and a dead man's toe."

I let out a surprised snorting laugh at the reference.

"But seriously, first, we need something of his."

"I have one of his shirts. Sometimes I wear it to bed."

"No. It can't be anything that could backfire on you."

"His grooming kit?"

"For fuck's sake. He has his own grooming kit here? What's even in it?"

"Hair gel, a special comb, moisturizer, and nail buffer, among other things."

The disbelief on her face is priceless, and I grab the kit out of the bathroom.

"I think the comb will work best since it probably has some of his DNA on it," Luna says when I return.

"What else do we need?" I ask.

"Carve Chad's name into one of those black candles." She hands me our carving tool, and when that's finished, I light it.

While I'm doing that, Luna sets about making the potion. She fills the cauldron with a combination of water and vinegar before adding some nightshade and quartz dust. To finish it off, she adds a squeeze of lemon, a dash of basil, and a pinch of patchouli.

"Now what?" I ask as I watch Luna stir. She's the pro here. I usually do only simple spells to make my life easier, like moving stuff when I don't want to get up, cooking and cleaning, and little parlor tricks like lighting candles. More just stuff around the house.

"Once it boils, we'll add in the comb and the melted wax from the candle. The last step is to write down the affliction we want him to have before throwing that in as well."

Nerves bubble in my stomach as I think about what we're about to do. I've definitely never done anything malicious like this before. I grab the pen and paper, preparing to write, but my hand starts shaking.

I hand them off to my sister. "You'll have to do it."

Her eyes glint. "You got it, babe."

"I'll be watching," I remind her, not wanting her to deviate from our plan.

"Spoilsport," she remarks as she writes "Chlamydia trachomatis."

Ten minutes later, the potion is bubbling, and we add in the final ingredients. It smokes and turns a sickly gray.

"Now what?"

"Now we wait."

I 'm lying in bed still fuming. I haven't been able to get one wink of sleep. That asshole fucked over my sister and deserves so much worse than what he got. I wonder if I would be able to do something more to him without Zara finding out. She would be so pissed at me if she ever learned that I did anything else behind her back. Well, that might be the wrong word, more like *disappointed*, but I just can't stand the thought of him getting away with this.

I'm a feisty bitch at the best of times, and I love fiercely. I don't have many in my circle who I would do literally anything for, but Zara is the *top* one. If I'm being honest, probably the *only* one. My little sister has always been innocent and in need of protection, although I know she would strongly disagree with me on that point. But even more, she *cares.* She has the biggest heart, and she deserves only the best. I hate that instead, she was cheated on by a fucking loser named Chad. I knew as soon as she told me his name that he would be a douchebag.

My heart breaks when I hear Zara crying through the walls. I wish I could make her feel better. Something she said earlier flits through my mind. *Aww, I wish I had a Binx of my own.* Maybe I should get her a cat. Too bad Chad isn't a cat. He's definitely a pussy.

I suck in a sharp breath. *Fuck, I'm brilliant.* I have the perfect way to get back at Chad, but to also make Zara feel better. A plan begins to form in my mind, and I'm itching to go get the spell book, but I have to wait until my sister is asleep. She can never know what I'm about to do. I quietly get out of bed and change, trying to get out my restless energy while I wait for her to pass out. I'll need to act fast.

Finally, after what feels like hours, her crying stops and I hear her soft snore that she lets out only when she's exhausted, sick, or has been bawling. I creep out of my room and into the Potion Pantry. I flip through the pages of the spell book and find exactly what I'm looking for. I remember coming across this spell recently, but I never thought I would be using it. I will be today. Nothing like testing a new spell on someone I don't give a shit about.

For as complex as this spell is, the process is actually fairly simple. The only thing that makes this dangerous is that I have to do blood magic, which I've never done before. Not until this douche.

I take a picture of the incantation so I don't have to bring the whole book with me, as well as a small pocket knife and a bowl that I use specifically for riskier spells. It's covered in protective runes that I etched myself.

With everything I need, I sneak out of the house. I'm grateful that when Zara started dating Chad, I had the foresight to have her send me his address. What can I say? I'm protective and want to make sure that my sister is safe.

I pull up the location and make the ten-minute drive over to his place. I expect all to be dark and quiet, but I do see a light on. I grab my things, and walk up to his door like I belong. That's where people tend to go wrong. If you look suspicious, that's when you run into trouble. I know this probably better than I should. I'm the troublemaker in the family after all.

I reach his front door only to find it locked. I release just a hint of my magic. Not enough for anyone to see, just enough to funnel into the lock. I hear it click and smile in victory. I enter, making sure to keep my steps quiet. I follow the sole light in the place, knowing it will lead me to him. I hear cursing and pained grunts coming from the bathroom, but no sign of the woman who was here earlier. Asshole probably fucked her after he dumped my sister and then sent her on her way.

The bathroom door is open when I round the corner, and Chad is butt-ass naked, facing away from me and hunched over himself. I scrunch up my face in disgust and confusion, but it finally clicks when he starts cursing.

"*Fuck*. What the hell is coming out of me?! And why does it *burn?*"

I almost start laughing, but somehow restrain myself. Looks like our spell worked. I still stand by my statement that it's not enough though.

"I bet that bitch gave me something," he mutters to himself.

"Hello, Chad," I purr.

He spins around in shock. I've never met him before, so he has no clue what I look like, and despite the fact that he's butt-ass naked and was just complaining about his dick burning and oozing, he gives me an appreciative once-over, lingering on my breasts. I roll my eyes. Maiden, I hate men. This is why I date women and only women.

"What can I do for you?" Classically thinking with his dick first. Not even concerned that some strange woman is in his apartment in the middle of the night. It seems to finally occur to him then. "How did you get in here?"

Before he can say or do anything else, like call the cops, even though I doubt he would with his reaction, I release my magic. The merlot-colored smoke pours from my fingertips, enveloping him. He lets out a panicked shout, but once my magic touches him, he's rendered immobilized. I need him to be still for the spell to work.

I walk up to him and I see fear coating his features. I give him a savage smile, dragging my pointed black nail over his cheek.

"You made a mistake when you cheated on my sister, Chad. You don't know who you've fucked with."

"I'm sorry!" he yells. "I'll make it up to her, I swear. Just please don't hurt me!"

I scoff at his promise. First off, there's nothing he could do to make Zara feel better. What is an apology going to do at this point? The only thing that will cheer her up is if she never has to see or hear from this asshole again, and if she has a new cat. Both things I can accomplish, and as an added benefit, he won't be able to hurt another woman this way ever again. Well, maybe some other cats once I finish my spell, but not another woman.

"I know you'll make it up to her. That's what I'm here to ensure. Don't worry, you'll be much less of an asshole soon enough."

I take the rune bowl out of my bag along with the knife. I set my phone down on the bathroom counter, bringing up the picture of the instructions.

I tune out the sound of his begging as I pick up the knife. I hold it to my palm, slicing it open and letting the blood pour into the vessel. The runes immediately start glowing and the scent of iron and magic permeates the air. An energy crackles through the room and I savor it.

With Chad still immobilized, I do the same to him and the feeling gets stronger, almost like an electrical storm. Maybe I should've done this in a bigger space. Oh well.

I dip my finger into the mixed blood before bringing it to the floor, drawing a circle around Chad. I then make the symbol for the Three-Faced Goddess—Maiden, Mother, and Crone, before finally marking his forehead with a pentagram as well.

"What are you doing to me? Please stop!"

I once again ignore him. I have bigger things to think about right now than pacifying him. I look at my phone to check the incantation, reading over it three times to make sure I have it right.

I close my eyes and hold my hands out in front of me again. Smoke pours from me as I speak.

"You must suffer your true fate
Mine you'll be in reincarnate
Pay the price for your crime
Forever live as a feline
Felis Catus
Felis Catus
Felis Catus"

I hold my breath. I've never done a spell like this before, and I'm nervous to see how it turned out. I peek one eye open and am delighted to see that it worked. A black cat sits in the middle of the circle and gives a soft meow. Much better than Chad's douchey voice.

I crouch down on the floor and release him from the immobilization magic.

"Here, kitty kitty," I coax.

He instantly walks over the boundary of the circle and approaches me. I'm prepared for him to attack me, but instead he just nuzzles my outstretched hand and gives a soft purr. I scratch his head a little and pick him up, and he lets me.

I read back over the spell and see that once they're changed, they don't retain any of their human memories or attributes. Perfect.

I do a quick spell to clean up my mess and then another to empty out his place, removing all furniture and belongings from his apartment. I grab his phone and cast a spell sending off a message to all his contacts that he's decided to relocate, change his number, and will no longer be in touch, ensuring our safety on the matter. We don't need anyone looking into the disappearance of Chad down the road and think we had anything to do with it. This way it looks like he just up and moved without a trace.

I've been here for a while now, and the sun is just beginning to peek out. I curse and collect Chad in my arms before making my way to my car. Zara will be up soon. She's always been a morning person and she doesn't tend to sleep well after situations like this.

I need an excuse as to why I was gone just in case she's already up when I get back. Coffee. Yes. Perfect. Zara loves herself some fancy-ass coffee with all the flavors in it.

I swing by our local coffee shop and get an iced coffee for myself and a hazelnut caramel frap for Zara, her favorite. I personally don't know how she drinks it, considering it could rot your teeth and give you diabetes from all the sugar. I also get us two breakfast sandwiches. I reluctantly decide to order a cup of whipped cream for Chad.

Ten minutes later when I'm back at home, I temporarily leave the cat in the car and bring in all the goodies. Sure enough, Zara is already awake.

"Where were you?"

"I thought I would surprise you with your favorite morning treats. I know you had a rough night last night and I thought this would make it a little better," I respond.

She has a sappy look on her face and I hope she doesn't start crying again. "Thanks, sister." She takes a grateful sip and sighs in contentment.

"I have another surprise for you. Wait here."

Without another word I head back out to my car to get Chad. When I walk through the door a minute later, I peek my head in. "Are you ready?"

"Yes! I'm dying to know what else you thought I could use at six in the morning."

Instead of responding to her smart-ass remark, I bring the cat inside.

Her mouth drops open in shock and then she squeals. Literally squeals. It's too early in the morning for that and I wince. I set him down and he immediately trots over to her. She picks him up and cradles him close. He nuzzles her and purrs. She lifts a teary gaze to mine, positively beaming.

Fuck yes. I knew this would be the perfect solution.

She comes over to me and wraps me in a Zara hug. I'm not usually a hugger, but I don't mind them from my sister.

"Where did you get him?"

Luckily I thought about this on the drive over and prepared an answer. "He was wandering the streets begging for food as I was getting us coffee."

"Aww, poor buddy. We'll take care of you and get you all the food you want. Don't you worry, Binxi." She smiles and looks up at me to see if I caught the name.

I laugh, but my smile quickly fades when there's a knock on the door. I frown at her.

I peek through the hole to see the newest acolyte, Genevieve, on the other side.

"What is the coven's newest grunt doing here?" I ask Zara.

Zara shrugs, but looks concerned. "What if it's about last night?"

"Eh. We're fine. I'm sure it's nothing serious. But there's only one way to find out."

I open the door.

"The coven needs to meet with you immediately," Genevieve says as soon as she sees me, and despite my reassurances to Zara, my stomach sinks a little.

THRee

Zara

We follow Genevieve through the set of wooden doors leading into our coven's official meeting room. I notice that only eleven of the thirteen candles used to signify each witch in the group are lit. *Shit, this can't be good.* I look at Luna with wide eyes, but she's fixated on the candles and doesn't notice me. Each member is seated at her place at the round table, but no one dares to look away from our high priestess, Serena.

As we go to take our usual seats, Serena's voice booms, "All rise."

Sweat beads at my forehead and my palms. This isn't at all how we typically do things around here.

I grab hold of the back of my chair and my eyes pin Serena. Her curly dark hair hangs in front of her eyes, and all I can see is her sparkly black lipstick.

"Luna. Zara." The air grows thick around us and no one dares to make a sound.

Luna inches her way closer to me, and I'm so thankful she's here with me right now. "Yes, Serena?"

"It has come to our attention that you've violated the rules of the coven. Therefore, you are both banned at once."

My jaw drops and a slight gasp escapes through my lips. *Violated the rules? What is she even talking about? From giving Chad an*

STD? Oh, come on! My thoughts won't stop questioning, but not a single word leaves my mouth.

"The fuck we have," Luna fights back, and I'm instantly met with relief.

"Excuse me, Luna. You have, indeed, and you both know we have a zero-tolerance policy when it comes to breaking our rules."

"Okay, then what rules did we break?" she snaps. "Or are you just going to continue to be vague?"

"We know what you did last night. Dark magic is not welcome here."

"Dark magic? Seriously? You're totally exaggerating," I say, finally speaking up.

Serena raises a hand. "That's enough of that. We are a highly coveted coven and will not tolerate rule-breaking and rude behavior."

"But—" I start to say, but I'm interrupted by Serena.

"Genevieve, please make sure these two see themselves out and begin to let the other candidates in one at a time. Thank you."

The nerve! This is totally unfair. Luna grabs my hand and squeezes it before pulling me behind her. Maybe she has more of an idea of what is going on.

We slowly make our way toward the door when I take a final glance back into the room. Everyone but Serena looks solemn but remains silent. It's a shame no one is trying to fight for us to stay. Or even asking questions.

I fight the urge to wave goodbye as we exit through the doors. Just outside of them, there is a line of at least twenty some odd witches.

"I will have you all come in for the interview process one at a time. Thank you for your patience and cooperation at this time," Genevieve says, and it's the loudest I've ever heard her speak.

We leave the building, but I feel so unsure of what to do next. Still holding my hand, Luna takes the lead until coming to a halt when we reach Full Bodied.

She's worked here for so long, we both find comfort in the space. We make our way over to our favorite chaise lounges, but before we even sit, she looks at me with her arms wide open, coming in for a big bear hug.

"You okay, Zar?" she asks while holding me.

I shrug. "Yeah, I'm fine, but what the hell? How could they do this to us?"

"I know, I don't get it either." She pulls away but her hands remain on my shoulders. "Seriously though, if they can drop us just like no big deal, then fuck them. We don't need them."

I nod before wiping a falling tear from my cheek. "You're right."

"And we still have each other. That's what matters."

As I let out a heavy sigh, my phone vibrates in my back pocket. "Hang on, Lu. I think I'm getting a phone call."

Her hands release me. "It better not be someone from the coven already asking for us to come back."

"I doubt it," I respond. I look down and see the word *Mom* lit up on the screen. "Worse... It's Mom."

Luna scoffs as I answer. She points toward the bar and mouths that she's going to get us a drink. I give a quick nod before answering the call.

"Hello," I say as cold as possible. Mom always calls me since she knows Luna won't ever answer, and I'm always the one who caves despite all the shit she's put us through over the years.

Without a proper greeting, I hear the words "Elizabeth is dead."

My heart stops beating for a brief second, and the world feels as though it's spinning around me.

"Did you hear me?"

"I'm sorry, what? Grandma's gone? That can't be."

"Zara, do you really think I'd waste my time calling you if it wasn't true? The celebration of life is at her house in Salem. Next weekend. Tell your sister. I've booked your flights. I'm going out early to get everything set up."

"But I thought you hated Grandma," I say.

"She's still my mother. And I'm yours. That's all. See you then." The phone goes silent and I see that she's ended the call.

"How'd that go?" Luna asks as she reappears with mimosas for us both. "Also, I know it's early, but after that shit I feel like we need a drink."

"Tell the boss. We're going to Salem next weekend."

Luna arches an eyebrow. "We are? Why?"

"Granny Lizzie died."

She gasps, cupping her hand around her mouth. "No."

Without another word, she plops down in the booth and tosses back her freshly poured drink.

Salem

After what felt like the longest flight ever, the cab pulls into the mile-long driveway that leads to our grandmother's house. We haven't been here in well over a decade, but its entire vibe matches that of the Salem Witch House from the seventeenth century. One difference is our grandmother always loved florals and bright colors, so the shutters are decorated with painted flowers and the brightest geraniums sit in the window boxes. The pop of color gives the dark house an inviting feel. Now that I think of it, that's how our grandma always felt too.

I swallow hard and release a big sigh. I wish Binxi were here with me right now, but I didn't want to travel with him just yet, especially for such a short trip. Luckily, Barb from the herb shop I work at is great with cats, so he'll be hanging out with her 'til we're back.

Luna hands me my suitcase from the trunk, and I stack my travel backpack on the top before I shut the cab door. When I turn around, my eyes meet Luna's. We exchange a brief nod of *We can do this* before making our way up to the front porch.

Luna is about to knock, but the door swings open. It's our mother.

"Hi, Mom," I say before giving an awkward wave. I have her dark hair and share a lot of her features, which I've always been a bit salty about.

Luna walks right past her without a word. I offer a polite smile before following behind her. When I'm out of the foyer and into the living space, I look around at a large crowd. It doesn't surprise me since Gran was always so kind to everyone she met. Before we have a chance to finish scanning the room, a girl around our age with red lipstick and a black nose ring that matches her jet-black hair approaches us.

"You must be Zara and Luna Arcana," she says. Her dimples and smile make her feel warm—a huge contrast to her dark look.

"We are," Luna answers, returning her smile. "Nice to meet you. What's your name?"

I blink twice before turning to look at Luna, wondering why she's being polite and smiling. Not that Luna is usually *rude*, but she is a bit abrasive and doesn't have patience for people. And I wouldn't say she's ever *friendly* to perfect strangers. She doesn't look back at me and keeps her eyes solely focused on the goth girl.

"Gwyn Tuttle. Well, just Gwyn. I was really close with Granny Lizzie." She leans in and hugs us both at the same time.

After her shockingly warm embrace, I stand there awkwardly.

"Well, 'Just Gwyn,' it's great to meet you," Luna says before touching her arm lightly.

Gwyn winks. "I'm so happy to meet you two finally. I've heard so much about you both from her. Kind of feels like I know you already. And she told me all about how you ladies practice magic like we do," she says excitedly before glancing toward the kitchen. "Well, now that we know each other, I'd love to introduce you to some people. They've been dying to meet you guys." She cringes for a second. "Oof, terrible word choice, but you know what I meant."

We both nod and follow Gwyn into the kitchen, where two girls and a guy are laughing and chatting as though they aren't at a funeral at all. I mean, I guess that's what Granny Lizzie would want—that's why this is a celebration of life. She never wanted people standing around complaining or wishing things were different. She simply wanted, and somehow successfully managed to do so, for people to see the simple joys in life and believe in the magic all around them.

Standing around the kitchen island, I first notice one of the girls laughing so hard she's snorting. Her hair is a gorgeous auburn red that frames her slightly freckled face. Her hand lands on the shoulder of a guy, and when I look to his face, his chestnut eyes lock with mine. Goose bumps make their way across my upper arms, stemming from the butterflies fluttering around in my stomach. He smiles at me and it feels as though we're the only two in the room. I smile back, about to give an awkward wave when I realize I'm right in front of the three of them now and he's holding out his hand for me to shake.

"Joey," he says with a crooked smile and a small dimple smack dab in the middle of his chin. He seems just as charming and panty-melting as my favorite *Friends* character and his namesake.

I place my hand into his, and warmth fills my body, shooting straight up to my cheeks. His handshake is firm, and it makes me feel safe.

Luna clears her throat next to me. "I think Joey's ready for you to let go now, Zar." I look over to Luna before blinking twice to rid the fog I was just in. I look back to Joey, and yes—I'm *still* holding his hand.

"Uh, yeah," I say before clearing my throat and finally freeing his hand from mine. "I am so sorry. I got caught up in the moment, I guess."

Luna smirks. "I'll say."

Gwyn points to the redheaded girl I first noticed. "Anyway, this is Hazel," she says before pointing to the other girl beside her with raven black hair and ice blue eyes, "and this is Morgan. They're witches too, and occasionally we will get together and practice magic."

I quickly shake both of their hands and offer up a polite "Nice to meet you."

Gwyn smiles. "Great, now that you've all met, I've got some other people to check on, so I'll be right back." She starts to walk away but turns around to add, "Oh, and hey, Zara and Luna, drinks on me at the Cauldron after this. Granny Lizzie insisted." She winks at us both, and I can't help but let out a small laugh. She's so cute, and I can already tell why she and Granny Lizzie were so close.

As Gwyn turns away for real this time, I notice a small shift in Luna's body language. She is totally into her. Too bad we won't be here for more than a couple days.

I glance back over to Joey, who is now chatting with an older gentleman.

Oh my Mother, he is so attractive. Shit. It's probably for the best that we aren't here much longer because I need a break from guys. As cute as he is, I don't need to make any more bad romantic choices after the whole Chad ordeal. I sure know how to pick them, and I absolutely cannot trust myself at all right now.

"We would love to hang out with you ladies sometime. Maybe we could even call the elements or something together, or, if you are pretty advanced, maybe we could teach each other some stuff?" Hazel asks.

"Yeah, we were able to do that for each other when we first started hanging out. Actually, Granny Lizzie introduced us and showed us some stuff too," Morgan chimes in.

"We loved her so much. Of course we grew up knowing we had magic and with our mothers teaching us, but they never took the time with us that your gran did," Hazel adds.

Tears spring to my eyes. That sounds like Gran. I wish we could've spent more time with her and been able to have had the kinds of experiences that these girls did.

We chat with them awhile, enjoying stories about their little group and our grandmother, but we can't shirk our duties for much longer.

Luna taps me on the shoulder, seeming to be of a similar mind-set. "Okay, ready to make the rounds and say hello to everyone?"

I look at all the strange, yet oddly familiar faces in the room. It feels like this is all some distant memory with how long it's been since we've seen Granny Lizzie, even though we were so close with her when we were younger. I take a deep breath and nod. "Yup, let's do this. And hey...sounds like we're in for some fun after this."

Luna smiles. "Agreed. Let's get this over with."

After an entire hour of mingling and hearing about how lovely and special Granny Lizzie was, we're ready to have some fun with Gwyn and her group of misfits. We find Gwyn, who has offered to drive us to the Cauldron.

We walk outside to our grandma's extended U-shaped driveway and follow Gwyn to a black Volkswagen Jetta.

"Wait, do you seriously drive a Jetta?" I ask since that's what Luna always drove before getting her Mini Cooper.

Gwyn glances between the two of us. "Yup, I seriously do. Why?"

"I used to drive one too, but just got a brand-new Mini that I love," Luna clarifies.

"Oh, cool," Gwyn says as she hops in the driver's seat.

I offer to take the back since I can tell Luna would love to sit up front with Gwyn. When we get in, Gwyn starts the engine and looks at me in the rearview mirror before giving me a smile. I return it and then look down and take notice that Luna's and Gwyn's elbows are touching on the center console.

"Girl, you drive stick shift too?" Luna asks.

"Hell yeah. Manual's the only way to go," Gwyn says.

They look at each other with understanding and smile before the car goes silent.

To avoid feeling like a third wheel, I decide to break the silence. "Okay, is there anyone in Salem that doesn't absolutely love and adore our grandmother? Or do people just say these kinds of things at funerals?"

Gwyn and Luna both start laughing.

"Of course, it's normal for people to say that kind of shit at funerals, but seriously, you guys had the best grandma around. She was like the entire town's grandmother. There was something about Granny Lizzie that just made people feel seen for who they were, and I don't think there is a soul out there who didn't love her."

My heart pangs a little to know that she was just as great as I remember, but we lost so much time with her. All because of our parents and their ridiculous closed-mindedness.

Before I can think more about it, Gwyn announces that we've arrived. I unbuckle my seat belt and get out of her car. As I shut the door, I look at what a tiny hole-in-the-wall this place is. "Guys, it's *so* cute!"

Gwyn and Luna laugh again, but this time they're both rolling their eyes at my excitement over this tiny bar with such a homey-looking feel.

We make our way over to a booth right next to the bar. The few people there are deep in their own conversations or taking sips out of their tiny cauldrons.

"The cups are cauldrons?" I ask.

"That's not even the best part," Gwyn says before winking at me.

Luna and I look at each other and exchange a smile. I take my seat in the booth and make sure not to scooch over all the way so that Luna will have to sit next to Gwyn. Once she realizes, she gives me a knowing smirk.

The bartender, a scruffy guy with tatted sleeves and a mustache, walks over to us from the bar.

"Hi, Gwyn, hi, ladies. I'm Marcus."

"Hi, Marcus," Luna and I say in unison.

"So, in celebration of our sweet Granny Lizzie, how about some shots on the house?"

All three of us shift our eyes back and forth from one another.

I'm not slightly surprised when Luna says, "Fuck it. Let's do it."

Gwyn laughs before telling Marcus, "Let's do one round now and then another when the rest of the crew gets here in about an hour."

"An hour? Are they not meeting us now?" I ask.

Before she can answer, Marcus shouts a quick "Coming right up" and heads back behind the bar.

Gwyn looks at Luna and then at me. "My friends are meeting us later because I wanted it to be just us girls first." She holds a finger in the air and says, "One second." Luna and I watch as Gwyn digs around in her bag until a dark gray envelope is in her hands.

She sets it down in the middle of the table and then puts her hands up in the air. "I'm not going to pretend I have a clue what it's about, and I don't know which one of you to give it to, so there it is."

I shift my eyes to Luna, hoping she knows what the hell is going on.

"Gwyn, what is it?"

"Oh, duh. Yeah, sorry for the dramatic effects there. It's a letter from Granny Lizzie to you both that she gave to me a few months ago and said, 'Look, honey, my time might be coming to an end, and if it does and you're still around here, please give this to my two sweet granddaughters.' She wanted me to give it to you after she passed, in person."

I stare at the envelope feeling unsure of what to expect. Money? Old birthday cards? Advice on how to deal with our mother?

"What do you think it is?" I ask Luna.

"Your guess is as good as mine. Want me to open it?"

I nod and slide it closer to her side of the table. She grabs it and opens it swiftly.

"Okay, it's definitely a letter."

Luna clears her throat to begin reading when Marcus returns with waters and three glass vials of potion. I arch my right eyebrow before asking, "What are those?"

"These are your shots," Marcus says. My eyes widen and I lightly clap my hands together in excitement over how cool everything here is. Before I can respond, Marcus asks, "Anything else I can get for you ladies right now?"

We shake our heads as Gwyn offers Marcus a thank-you before looking back to us. Luna tucks the letter away to the side and grabs one of the vials.

"This place is seriously so cute. We love witchy stuff, so this is right up our alley."

"Right? This place is one of my favorites. It's a local fav too, and not a lot of tourists know about it, which makes it even better." Gwyn grabs the remaining two vials, hands me one, and raises hers up in the air. "Cheers, bitches."

"Cheers," I say and hold my vial close to Gwyn's. My typical dread before taking a shot isn't there for some reason today.

"Cheers," Luna begins. "To the best grandma ever, to my wonderful sister, and to adventures with new friends."

"Abso-fucking-lutely," Gwyn says and all three of us clink our vials together before slugging them back.

My mouth puckers at the taste of lavender, lemon, and vodka as the shot burns its way down my throat. I usually refuse any offers to take a shot, but today, it just feels right. Setting the vial down, I ask, "All right, sis. Are you ready to do the honors?"

Luna releases a loud sigh before shaking her head. "I don't know if I'm ready, but I'm super curious to read what might be her final words to us."

"Same," I say. "You've got this, babe."

She gives me one last reassuring wink before reopening the letter.

My dearest Luna and Zara,

If you girls are reading this, it means I have finally kicked the old bucket after all these years. I want to start by saying I am so proud of the two of you. Defying your mother's expectations by branching out on your own was quite the feat. You followed your hearts and forged your own paths, and I couldn't have been happier to know that you both have found your strength and kept true to who you really are.

Because of this, it is my wish and would mean the world to me if you took over my apothecary shop, Enchanted Elixirs, here in Salem. I'm sure we all can agree had I left it to your mother she'd probably burn it to the ground. I trust you two more than I do myself, and so I know if this is something you take on, it will flourish in ways I could only imagine. Not only am I leaving you the shop, but assuming you'll need a place to stay, the house is all yours as well.

Oh, and one more thing—if you do stay, please make sure my Gwynnie has a job at the apothecary until she finally learns she really doesn't need me or the shop and goes and opens her own one day. Also, I know deep in my heart the three of you are bound to hit it off, and it fills me with joy to know that you'll all have each other.

It's been so lovely that we've stayed in touch for all of these years, and my only regret was not being able to visit you in Manitou Springs. I believe this is my final life here on Earth as I have no more left to uncover, but I hope you both know my love and magic are all around and within you.

Believe in yourselves as I believe in you.

All my magical love,

Granny Lizzie

Tears flood our eyes as soon as Luna reaches the end of our grandmother's written words. We hold out our hands across the table and grab them as if we're about to do an incantation. Instead, we each squeeze each other's hands and feel Granny Lizzie's presence wrap around us. I close my eyes and imagine she's with us now, leaning in for a great big hug. When I open them, Marcus is at the table with tissues for all of us. We giggle and thank him before he turns around.

"Well, that was unexpected. I hope it's okay that I heard all of that," Gwyn says.

I wipe at a falling tear. "It's more than okay. I think it's safe to say that was her plan all along."

"Yeah, Gwyn. It really means the world to me—us—that Granny Lizzie had you here with her all this time. We appreciate you so much."

"Seriously, girl. Thank you," I chime in.

Gwyn waves her hand at us. "Oh, hush. It's not a big thing. She was the only grandmother I've ever had. I owe her the whole fucking moon."

"Yeah, we do too," Luna says. We all sit in silence for a moment before I start to reflect on what was written. *Move to Salem? Own an apothecary? Move into our grandmother's home?* It's a lot to process, and I wonder what Luna's thoughts are. Before I ask, it hits me that I don't really have anything in Manitou that I'd miss. As long as I'd have Luna and Binxi, a fresh start actually sounds...exciting.

Luna's eyes find mine, and I can feel that she's had the same thought.

"Well, sis. We movin' to Salem or what?" she asks.

I take a look around the cute, witchy bar then to Gwyn before my eyes land back on my sister.

"As long as Binxi comes too," I say and flash her a smile.

Luna smiles back at me before cupping her hand to one side of her face and yelling, "Marcus, we're gonna need another round over here, please."

Three weeks later...

I take a sip of wine as I unpack *another* box. I sigh in regret. This is my last bottle that I brought from Full Bodied. So far, Salem has been wonderful, but there are definitely some things that I miss about our old life. Namely, getting wine whenever I want for half price.

Zara seems to be on the same wavelength as me as I hand her another mug. You would think that we have enough, but between the two of us, we have an abundance. Mine are all witty, bitchy, and sarcastic, just like me. Zara's are all cutesy and happy. Then, of course, we have a million witchy mugs that we both use. We always say we're not going to buy any more, and then one of us will come home with a new one.

"I'm going to miss this wine when we inevitably run out," she comments.

"This is our last bottle, so enjoy it while you can."

"What? Nooooo. It's my favorite," she whines, and Binxi rubs against her in response to her distress.

I inwardly chuckle to myself. In the last few weeks, she has fallen in love with him. I feel a little bad not telling her that it's actually her ex who cheated on her and who we gave an STD. But, at this point, he's finally making her happy, and I don't have the heart to tell her. At least not yet. There's no reason to. Maybe there never will be.

"Maybe I can call Zach and convince him to send us more. He always did have a thing for me, even though I've never been into men and he knew it."

"I think he was convinced he could turn you straight," Zara remarks with a smirk.

I shudder. "I can't even..." Another shiver works its way down my spine at the thought of sleeping with a man. Especially a man like Zach.

I look around the house. Granny Lizzie's house. I guess I shouldn't be shocked that she didn't leave anything to my parents. Our mother turned away from the craft a long time ago. She found my dad, who has always been deeply religious. My mother fell in love and he started bringing her to church, and after that, she wanted nothing to do with the coven. The last time we saw our grandmother, we were ten and eleven. She had taken us to our awakening ceremony under the full moon. Our color magic awoke, and when our mother found out that my grandmother had taken us without her permission, she up and left Salem, moving us across the country and cutting off all contact with her. We moved to Colorado Springs for two reasons: it was far from my grandmother's reach, and it was a religious city.

My sister and I practiced our own magic in secret until Zara turned eighteen. She's younger than I am by a year, so I wanted to wait for her. We moved to Manitou Springs, the first and closest witchy city we could find. My parents were not happy with us, to say the least. Over the years, Zara and I have talked about coming out for a visit to see Granny Lizzie, but we've always been too busy, and Gran has always seemed so young and healthy. We never thought that she would pass and the choice would be taken from us before we were able to see her as adult witches. And she has always had a fear of flying, saying something about not trusting those modern contraptions. We spoke with her plenty on the phone. Hell, she's how we acquired our first spell book.

Considering that we're her only relatives who have the same lifestyle she did, not to mention the only ones she was in contact with, I shouldn't be surprised that she left everything to us. It still baffles me though. Partly because her death was so unexpected. Well, apparently we were the only ones not expecting it since Gran told Gwyn she thought her time was coming. A bit of anger burns in my chest that she didn't confide in us about that. We would've made it a priority to come out and see her.

"Do you feel weird living here?" I ask Zara. "We haven't been here since we were young, but it hasn't changed in the slightest. It still feels like *her* house. I get it hasn't been that much time yet, but I feel a little creeped out being surrounded by all her things."

"Yeah, maybe a little. I would feel bad changing stuff though. It's like we're disrupting her memory or something, don't you think?"

"Here's the thing. She's gone. She left this place to us, and the apothecary. I think she would want us to be comfortable and make the spaces our own. I don't want to constantly feel like I'm treading on her memory by wanting to move something or put our own decorations up."

Zara gets a little furrow between her brows, her face conflicted. "That makes sense. I'm sure you're right. What do you want to do with all of this stuff, then?"

"Well, I do like a lot of it. Maybe we can just start by donating what we don't like, and then rearranging what we want to keep. Also, keep in mind that we can always bring stuff to the apothecary if we don't want it here, and vice versa."

She nods. "As much as I love this house, I do miss our old apartment."

I give her a sad smile. "I do too. Honestly, I think making this space feel more like our own will really help with that though. Let's take a break from unpacking and figure out what we do and don't want."

She nods enthusiastically. We make our way around the house, slowly going through everything. Zara takes everything off the walls with her bubblegum-pink color magic and a sweep of her hand. I follow behind her cleaning the area and the walls and surfaces with my red-wine color magic. It's painstaking, but it's also kind of fun. It feels like we're breathing new life into this space. We open all the windows and get some fresh air into the house, and make it nice and bright. We smudged the house with sage as soon as we moved in, but it could probably use another one soon. I like to do that frequently after moving into a new space to clear out the old energy.

We form three piles. One, donate. Two, keep in the house. Three, move to the shop. Our donation pile is by far the biggest, and it feels refreshing to be getting rid of excess stuff that we don't want or need here.

We load pile one into our cars so it's out of the house, and I'm already breathing easier. Then, we combine pile two with our own decor that we have yet to put up. With everything off the walls and shelves, it will be easier to figure out how we want to arrange everything. I know the third pile is going to have to wait until we're ready to redecorate the apothecary, which we aren't quite ready to start yet. That one is actually going to be an even bigger project than the house. For now, we put the pile by the door for when we *are* ready to do that.

The apothecary has been closed since Gran died, but we have plans to reopen it. Luckily, Gwyn knows how she operated everything. My heart beats harder when I think of her, and I can feel a blush creeping up my cheeks. Zara notices immediately, considering it's unusual behavior for me.

"What's wrong? You look flushed."

"Nothing. I'm fine."

She scrutinizes me closely, and I wave her off, annoyed she can see I'm flustered.

"This wouldn't have anything to do with a certain gorgeous emo employee, would it?"

I scoff, but I don't have it in me to deny her. There's a connection between Gwyn and me that I haven't felt in a long time. I could tell when we went out to the Cauldron after the funeral that she felt the same way. Our hands would brush, or we would give each other subtle little touches. The current that seemed to run between us had my breath catching with every graze of our skin.

I attempt to somewhat change the subject to what I was thinking before Gwyn popped into my head. "We'll have to do the apothecary next. It's going to need just as much work, if not more so. We need to make it a bit more modern. As much as I loved Granny Lizzie, she was definitely dated. We want to bring in not only the locals, but tourists as well."

Zara nods, letting my subject change fly. "Maybe next week when we're more settled we can tackle that."

"How would you feel about having a girls' night there while we drink some wine and blast some music with the girls from the funeral? They mentioned they'd be more than willing to help us out with that."

She gives me a knowing look, but I'm grateful when she doesn't say what I know she's thinking. "Well, we *could* use the extra sets of hands."

"Yes. And it would be handy to have Gwyn around. She knows that place like the back of her hand."

Zara looks as though she's about to smile, but once again refrains. "I think that would be a good idea."

"I'll text her then and see if she can wrangle the other girls in."

Gwyn and I exchanged numbers after the funeral. For the logistical aspect, of course.

> Hey girl, it's Luna. Would you and the girls be willing to help us revamp the apothecary? It's going to be a lot of work and we need all hands on deck.

> I know it's you. We exchanged numbers, remember? And I would love to. I've been dying to redecorate that place for ages. I'll text Morgan and Hazel.

Maiden, Mother, Crone, I love her sass and snark. Honestly, it's right on par with my own. We are going to definitely keep each other occupied.

Well, no one ever forgets me. *wink emoji*

You are pretty unforgettable.

Oh, Mother, I'm already swooning. I'm in deep shit with this one.

Next Friday then?

Yes. The girls are in too.

Perfect. See you then. We'll bring the wine.

You might need to send me a picture of yourself. Just so I know for sure I'm texting the right person.

I laugh aloud. I love that she's teasing me even though she already told me I was unforgettable. I turn my camera on and send her a picture of my bare feet, which both have witchy tattoos on them, by the way—a crescent moon with a broom on one, and a black cat on the other, her tail winding around my ankle.

Sexy. And just who I thought you were.

*I didn't realize you had a foot fetish. I'll make sure to keep them well groomed for you, darling. *kissy wink emoji**

That settled, I set my phone down, an enormous smile on my face, only to see that my sister is staring at me.

"What?"

"Oh, nothing at all. I just don't think I've ever seen you smile for anyone like that other than me."

"I wasn't smiling."

"Sure. Whatever you want to tell yourself. What did she say?"

I almost tell her to mind her own business, but then realize she's asking about setting up the apothecary.

"Next Friday. The girls are coming too."

"That's what she said."

I make a shocked sound. "Zara Ann Arcana. Did you just steal my joke?"

She rolls her eyes at me but laughs all the same.

"Let's finish getting the house set up, then, if that's only like a week away," Zara says, and we get back to work.

We spend the week organizing, smudging some more, and filling the house with *us.* Slowly but surely it starts coming together and feeling more like ours. Binxi makes himself at home too, finding his favorite spots to lounge in. Zara is insistent we clear off some spaces high above for him to roam.

"Cats need to be high up. It's in their nature. I watched a show about it once. If they don't have what they need, they get sad and mean."

I scoff. Leave it to Zara to watch a fucking cat show.

"Did you watch this before or after we got him?"

"Does it matter?"

"Yes."

She huffs. "Before," she admits reluctantly, making me laugh.

The next week, we meet the girls at the apothecary. I look up at the dilapidated sign. *Enchanting Elixirs* is written above the shop, but it's faded and the *E* in Elixir is hanging extremely precariously. I make mental notes of everything that needs to be updated and dealt with. The building itself is gorgeous. Red and brown brick make up the entirety of it and speak of its old-world charm. Gran had this place forever.

We make our way inside to see Gwyn already behind the counter, as if she's so used to being there that's where she automatically gravitates. Her green eyes lock on mine as the bell chimes above the door, signaling our entry. My breath catches as we stare at each other, and she's the first to look away, moving her gaze to my sister.

I look around the shop, taking everything in with new eyes, thinking about what we're going to do with the place. The walls are a dingy cream, and I'm not sure if they were always that color or if they used to be white and have years of caked-on dirt and grime. The shelves and counters are all crowded with tons of products and herbs. It's common for apothecaries, but it feels like there's too much. The lighting is low, slightly outdated, and covered in cobwebs. Fitting, but at the same time, it needs to be improved. I don't want to have a dirty shop.

"Hey, ladies. It's so nice to see you again! How have things been? Settling in okay?" she asks.

I nod. "We're getting there. We've mostly got the house how we want it, but this has been weighing on us. It'll be nice to have help getting it all sorted before we do our grand reopening."

"Yes! Thank you so much for your help. We really appreciate it." Zara looks at me before continuing. We talked about this before we came here, making sure we were both on the same page. We want to make all business decisions together. I give her a nod. "Actually, we wanted to see if you'd be willing to continue working here after we get it up and running? We really like you and you know more about this shop than we do."

Gwyn's face lights up. "Oh really? I was hoping you'd ask me. I know that your gran asked you to keep me on, but I wasn't sure if you'd want to have employees or not. I loved Granny Lizzie and this shop so much. I've been looking for a job just in case, but I'm so glad I can stay here." She runs over and wraps me in a tight hug. I'm not usually very touchy with people, but I enjoy her touches more than I thought I would. Her cinnamon and sugar scent hits me and I inhale it deeply into my lungs. Maiden, I could get addicted to that. She pulls away to give Zara a hug, and I reluctantly let her go.

"So, when are Morgan and Hazel getting here?" I ask after they pull apart.

"They can't show up until later, so in the meantime, I thought the three of us could go through the inventory and see what you both want to keep and get rid of as well as what you'd like to add."

We nod and she starts taking us through the shop. She's very knowledgeable on the inventory—what products sell well and which ones don't. We follow her lead on what items we should either get rid of or keep a very limited supply of. She also has some suggestions for things we should add to the shop. She brought some of them up to Gran a while back, but she was resistant to a lot of new things. She liked doing things a more old-fashioned way. The shop wasn't huge with tourists, which is understandable, but it's a potential huge business increase. We decide to have a little more kitschy section designed for people who don't really know what they're doing, or just want a memento from Salem.

"What if we have little potions or something that are already premixed and bottled? I bet people would eat that shit up," I chime in. I could make legit potions. They would be very subdued and not at their full potency, but I bet they would do really well.

"Well," Gwyn says quietly, leaning in as if to tell us a secret, even though we're the only ones here. "Granny Lizzie actually did have regulars come in that she discreetly made potions for."

My eyebrows fly up. This is news to me. "Well, we can keep that going if they're willing to buy from us instead."

She nods and writes something down in her notebook. From what I can tell, she's very well organized.

A few hours later, Hazel and Morgan show up. We all get our glasses of wine, and I connect my music to the sound system. We've also ordered a pizza, which should be here soon. By this time, we have established a plan. Honestly, it's similar to the one we came up with for the house, but with more organization, thanks to Gwyn. We start by taking everything off the shelves and the walls and forming piles. We considered using our magic, and we do a little bit, but with so many of us here, it would get too dangerous and chaotic.

The items are divided by category, which Gwyn is overseeing. Then, everything will be thoroughly cleaned, and after we've sorted through all the merchandise, we will paint and everything will go back onto the walls and shelves.

We get to work, assigning each girl to a task. With five of us, it's moving pretty quickly. Gwyn is organizing everything that we bring her into her little system, and the remaining four of us make relatively quick work of the shop.

I'm working on the book section when I notice a smudge on the silver crescent moon embedded in the shelf. I wipe my thumb over the moon when the shelf swings inward and I suck in a sharp breath.

"Maiden, Mother, Crone. Ladies, you all need to come here right the fuck now. I've just found something."

They all crowd around me, Zara first since she was closest. I hear their gasps of surprise as we look down the stairwell that leads to a dusty and dank corridor.

"How did you do this?" Gwyn asks, and I can see she's more shocked than anyone. That answers my unspoken question of if she knew about this or not.

"I just rubbed my thumb over the little moon."

"Maiden, I've done that a million times and it's never happened for me. I wonder if it's somehow spelled to open for just the two of you."

I look over at my sister, her eyes just as wide as mine feel.

"Let's go see what Gran has in store for us," I say, turning on the flashlight on my phone.

Zara looks hesitant, but I don't let her chicken out. I grab her hand and we descend into the depths of the shop. There are cobwebs leading down the stairs, and even though the passageway should feel creepy, instead I feel a sense of comfort.

When we finally reach the bottom, candles spring to life around us, as though on a motion sensor. That's a nifty spell. I wish I knew what it was.

The chamber around us is circular, and when I glance down at the floor, I see a pentagon. There's a table in the middle of the space with a single book lying on it that's illuminated by something. I look up and gasp. Somehow there's a skylight and the moon is shining directly inside. Mother, I love magic.

We carefully approach, not sure of what other spells might be at work here. Zara and I reach for the book at the same time, and when we do, a shimmering blue smoke emanates from it. I would be worried, but I instantly recognize my grandmother's magic. It brushes up against me and my sister like a warm spring day, just like Granny Lizzie.

When nothing else happens, we attempt to open the book and come across no issues. I'm fairly certain the magic we sensed and saw was a protection spell in case someone other than us tried to read it.

Moon Temple Coven

Elizabeth Arcana
Ruth Tuttle
Mary Stonecroft
Winnie Stonecroft

Sarah Stonecroft
Briar Forsythe
Blair Forsythe
Sparrow Eastey
Tabitha Calderone
Raven Darkhaven
Lydia Fata
Sage Cunningham
Delphi Maxia

"Oh shit," I say, looking over the list. "I think this was Gran's original coven. But this book looks old. Like older than makes sense."

I look around at the other girls before handing it off for them to inspect. Gwyn takes it first.

"All of our ancestors are on this list," she points out quietly.

Morgan looks at it first. "Delphi Maxia," she says reverently, tracing her name with her finger.

Hazel leans over her shoulder murmuring, "Raven Darkhaven."

"Who's yours, Gwyn?" I ask. I think I know, but I want to be sure.

"Ruth. Rue Tuttle. She was very close with your grandmother." She gives me a look I can't quite decipher. I want to ask her about it but she subtly shakes her head at me. Later, then.

"Joey and Arthur's ancestors are on here too. Blair and Briar Forsythe. Although I'm not sure which one. Oh and Allegra's," Morgan comments.

"Who's Allegra?" Zara asks.

Hazel rolls her eyes. "Arthur's girlfriend. Her ancestor is Tabitha Calderone."

"I take it you're not a fan," I notice.

"Allegra is different. She's always been kind of bitchy and it's like she's always trying to seduce everyone," Morgan answers for her.

"But she has a boyfriend?" Zara asks.

"Yes. And as far as we know, she's never been unfaithful, but she always just has this way about her that attracts the wrong kind of attention."

"I see," I remark. It sounds to me that men like her because she's beautiful, while other women dislike her for it. Honestly, I bet we will get along fine.

"How do we know that all of these people are actually descendants? Maybe it's a coincidence," Zara asks. Mother bless her naive little soul.

"It's no coincidence. All of these families have been in Salem since the witch trials. They were some of the only witches to survive that time," Gwyn says.

My heart starts pounding. This isn't just a coincidence. This all feels like fate. There's something larger at play here. I can feel it in my witchy bones.

I look around at the women. "What do you ladies think? Want to form our own coven?"

Zara

I stare at the list of the Moon Temple Coven names before nodding a yes to my sister. It's unbelievable how we all connect like this. And to have our own coven. Shit, that sounds amazing. Chills shoot down my spine as I look around at the rest of the girls.

"We should totally reach out to some of the descendants to see if they'd want to join us," I suggest to the group.

"Yes, definitely. I was thinking something similar. Good idea, Zar," Luna says. Her approval always means so much to me since I'm usually a bit slow when it comes to these things.

I run my finger across the names when Gwyn clears her throat. "I hate to be the bitch here, ladies, but aren't we supposed to be updating this place? I've been dying to get it cleaned up and revamped since we all know Granny Lizzie was a tad old school, and I don't want us to lose momentum."

Luna leans her shoulder on mine. "She's right. Why don't we come back to this idea and we can split up the names to research and go from there?"

I take a deep breath and nod. "Yeah, you guys are right. That sounds like a good idea to me."

After one more glance at the book in my hand, I close it and put it back on the middle of the table just as it was before. We all begin to migrate back to the stairwell that leads to the main shop area. As Luna closes the passageway so it returns to its bookshelf-looking self, someone knocks on the door. I release a scream as Luna and I both jump.

"Guys, it's just the pizza getting delivered," Morgan says, laughing. She grabs it from the delivery guy before setting it on the coffee table.

"Guess it's safe to say we're both still in our heads about what we just found," I mumble to Luna. She nods slowly before making her way over to the pizza box and grabbing a slice. I follow behind her and grab one too.

As I take a bite of the delicious and fresh pizza, the cheese melts right out of the side of my mouth. Damn it, I need a napkin. I hold my hand up to my mouth, and when I see the roll of paper towels from across the room, I flick my fingers to conveniently tear one piece off and bring it straight to me. I'm finally getting more comfortable using my magic—even if it is just simple, convenient magic—around here.

The paper towel reaches my hand and I wipe my mouth. Out of the corner of my eye, I spot a figure in the shadows. The energy of the room shifts and the temperature plummets. I can feel eyes on me, and I remain still before turning my head. When I do, no one is there. Hmm, that's odd. I take another bite of pizza when the figure reappears. I quickly turn my head again, but still no one. Maybe it's just a trick of the light.

"Zar, you okay over there?" Luna asks.

"I'm honestly not sure. I keep feeling like someone is staring at me, but no one's there."

She lets out a chuckle. "I think we're just all a little spooked about knowing that there is a hidden passageway that no one ever told us about."

"Yeah, true." I wave the paper towel I'm holding to make it appear like I don't care, but seriously, that was creepy as fuck. I inhale and close my eyes for a second before opening them and scarfing down the rest of the slice of pizza.

"I'm going to go wash my hands, and then I'll be ready to get back to decorating," I announce. The girls all chime in with "Same here."

I head to the small bathroom in the back of the shop and scrub my hands with honey lavender soap. After drying my hands, I decide to start working on organizing the herbs since they're so calming to me. Knowing how many benefits they have and the natural power they hold is so inspiring to me. I make my way over to the Workshop—the section of the shop where we prepare all the herbs, potions, and oils. On the way, I notice a bunch of old figurines that look like they've sat in the same position for over a hundred years. Two of them stare deeply into my soul. When I get close to one, I swear it looks like she's smiling at me.

"Hey, everyone," a familiar deep voice calls out, stealing my attention from the creepy figurines. I've only just met him and I already recognize Joey's voice. As I turn around to smile and wave, he continues, "We heard you could use a little help around here?"

We. And when I see him, I see her too. I stop for a moment to catch my breath since for some strange reason it feels like the wind was knocked out of me.

She's shorter than I am, platinum blonde with dark roots, and her whole body looks like she's lived in a tanning salon. I couldn't even guess her age if I tried since her lips, nose, eyelashes, eyebrows, and, well, entire face have definitely all had work done. Despite her resemblance to a knock-off Barbie doll, a pang of jealousy surges through my chest. I do feel bad that I'm critiquing her looks so much. If she is Joey's girlfriend, I bet she's actually really sweet and kind. I'd never judge someone based on their looks, and I certainly have no right to start doing so with this girl.

"Hi," I say before awkwardly waving at her.

She squints her eyes at me with the bitchiest look. *What the hell?*

"Oh, I'm so rude. Sorry, Zara, this is Tiffany. Tiffany, Zara."

I extend a hand and she does as well before using hers to flip her hair over her shoulder. "Um, hi."

"Well, come on in," I offer. Looking to Tiffany, I ask, "I was just about to organize some of the herbs and set up our healing boxes. Wanna help?"

Her mouth opens, but instead of responding, she lifts a finger to me as she uses her other to pull her phone from her back pocket. She shrugs. "Sorry, I can't. Gotta take this."

I give her a half smile before she walks over to a corner nearby to talk.

Joey inches closer to me. "I don't mind helping with herbs. I mean, I don't know shit about them, but I'm happy to do whatever you tell me."

Oh? I can't help the flutter that arises in my stomach... and other parts.

"Um, sure," I say before clearing my throat. "That'd be great. If you want to follow me, I'll take you back to the Workshop."

Joey hesitates for a moment as Tiffany walks over to him.

"Everything okay?" he asks her. The tone of his question packs so much concern that a wave of jealousy courses through my veins again. *He has a girlfriend*, I remind myself. One standing no fewer than three feet from me at that. Good Mother, what is going on with me lately?

My thoughts are interrupted by Tiffany's whine. "Babyyyy, you won't believe it. Brittney's boyfriend broke up with her and she's just devastated."

"Hasn't it only been like three weeks?"

I cup my hand across my mouth to stifle a laugh. Joey's eyes flicker to mine before returning to Tiffany.

She scoffs. "It doesn't matter. Her heart is broken. I'm going to go over and check on her." She looks at me for a second before planting a kiss on him in front of me. "Toodles," she says before practically sprinting out the shop door.

I stand there staring at Joey. He stares back and shrugs before offering, "Sorry she had to take off."

"Understandable. No problem. Are you leaving too, then?" I ask.

Joey places his hands in his pockets and looks around the shop before his eyes meet mine again. "Nah, we've got some herbs to organize, right?"

Heat rises in my cheeks as I flash him a smile. I nod. "Right. Follow me."

I lead the way to the Workshop feeling his eyes upon my backside. It gives me the boost of confidence I haven't felt since before Chad. I turn around briefly and his eyes quickly move away from my ass to my eyes. His cheeks redden. "I'm still here," he says.

"I see that," I remark as I use my body to push open the door to the Workshop. "Well, here we are. These are the potions and oils here and back this way is where all the herbs are."

"Oh, very nice," he says. "So what do we need to do exactly?"

"Basically, just get everything cleaned up a bit and make them presentable for sale. Some are in the fridge, some are drying out, and the ones that are dried I need help packaging and labeling so we can sell them. Once they're ready, we set them up in different types of self-care or healing boxes like those over there." He nods along as I go through the rest of the directions. "Any questions?"

"Nope, I think I got it. I'm ready."

"Quick learner," I quip.

He smiles. "Well, I do have a good teacher after all."

Oh my Mother, is this boy seriously flirting with me? As bad as it sounds, I don't want him to stop. I need to do my usual routine to regain focus. I snap my fingers to signal the twelve candles I set up earlier to light at once. Something about candles always helps put me in a good workflow.

Joey gasps, reminding me that he's present and just witnessed me snap my fingers to set a bunch of candles aflame.

"Are those some kind of Clapper candles called Snappers or some shit?" he asks.

I giggle. "Yeah, something like that. I have a lot of things set up to make my life a little easier, especially for mundane tasks." The thought of him attempting to do it on his own has me chuckling to myself.

He nods. "Makes sense. Efficient." He starts to look around at the Workshop table. "Wait, where are the jars that go in the boxes?"

"Oh, right. Let me get them down for us." I wave my hand and point to an empty spot on the table, and the tall cabinet in the corner of the room opens and multiple jars float down to the table. Pink smoke trickles around the room.

When it clears, I see Joey looking amazed, but not surprised.

"Yeah, I've got a couple, er—tricks I can do."

His lips purse and eyes squint for a moment. "Oh, you're just like the other girls, aren't you?"

"What's that supposed to mean? I'm like the other girls?"

"Shit. My bad. I didn't mean it that way. I meant that you're..." He pauses before changing his voice to a whisper, "Magical."

I laugh. "Yes, I am...magical," I whisper back with a wink.

"Hah, sorry. That probably made me sound like the biggest dork. I'm low-key jealous of y'all. I feel like there's nothing about me that's special or unique."

My lips form a pout. "Aw, Joey, don't say that. You are special and unique simply by being you. I know we just met, but I seriously feel the great energy that you have and give off."

"Oh yeah?" he asks.

"Yeah."

"Thanks," he says before clearing his throat. "Okay, now that I've finished putting one of these boxes together, how's this look?"

"Absolutely perfect," I say. He smiles wide and I can tell he's feeling proud of himself.

Time to focus, I remind myself, before taking a deep breath. Before I tie a small ribbon around one of the self-love boxes, I decide to add a crystal. I reach for a rose quartz at the same time Joey reaches for a jar, and his hand grazes mine. An electric current flows through my body. We lock eyes but say nothing. His eyes shift down to my lips.

"You guys!" Luna bursts through the Workshop door, and I thank the Three-Faced Goddess for the interruption.

"What's going on?" I ask.

My sister pauses to catch her breath. "Sorry, I'm so excited. Come out here so I can share the news with the others too."

We follow her out to the main shop floor and she announces, "I found another descendant who lives here!"

"What?! That's awesome!" I say.

Gwyn moves closer to us. "You just couldn't fucking wait, could ya?" Her tone is stern but she flashes Luna the sweetest smile I've ever seen and winks.

"Luna is seriously so impatient," I add.

"Duly noted," Gwyn says. "Did you at least finish dusting the rest of the shelves?"

"Of course I fucking did. And I even rearranged and organized three of the cabinets for the potion stock. So, I figured I had a few minutes to do some digging online and see what other descendants we could possibly meet here."

Joey looks at me. "Descendants?"

I look to Luna, who gives me a "can we trust this dude?" look. I give her a gentle reassuring nod, and her raised eyebrow lowers.

"Yeah, here. Follow me, and I'll show you the coolest fucking thing we found earlier." Without thinking, I grab Joey's hand and lead him to the hidden passageway. When we make our way down the staircase, he stops and takes in his surroundings.

"Holy shit. This is awesome."

"Right?" I nod in excitement. "We found it earlier today, and there's something even more awesome." I reach for the journal from the center of the round table and turn to the page of the listed coven members. I tilt it toward him and his eyes grow large when he sees "Forsythe" listed.

"Whoa. I have goosebumps." He rubs at his arms. "Artie is going to shit his pants when he finds out about this."

"He's your brother, right?"

"Yeah. Our last name is Forsythe." He runs his forefinger underneath each name listed. "There are other ones here that I recognize too. I'm pretty sure that Artie's girlfriend, Allegra Calderone, is one too."

"Yeah, that's what Gwyn mentioned earlier," Luna adds.

"We were thinking of starting our own coven, actually," I say. Joey looks to me and Luna.

"Just us girls though," Luna says, and I cringe.

He puts both hands in the air. "Totally get it. You all are the ones with the magic anyway, so that makes sense."

"Which is why we'd have it be an all-girls thing," I say, hoping to soften the blow of Luna's matter-of-fact statement.

"Well, I'd love to help if you'd like. In fact, I can introduce you guys to Allegra."

"That'd be so great," I say.

"Maybe you two could do that tomorrow. I'm going to finish researching some of these others, so it'd be nice to have some help with finding the girls," Luna says.

Joey looks at me and gives a reassuring nod. "Yeah, for sure. I'll text Artie now. Want to do coffee with them first thing tomorrow morning?"

"It's a date," I say. "Well, not a *date* date, but I'll add it to my calendar," I add, trying to save myself from my damn awkwardness.

"I know what you mean," he chuckles. I can feel my cheeks turning pink and look to Luna to ground myself.

"Okay, we'll meet Allegra tomorrow, and I'll see if she's interested in joining the coven. Anyone else I should reach out to?"

"Yes. I just found an Evanora Fata who lives at 78 Chestnut St."

"I know exactly where that is," Joey says. "It's only a few blocks from the coffee shop we can meet Artie and Allegra at."

"Sounds like a plan. Can you text me the address so I can meet you there?" I ask him.

"I'll just swing by and pick you up at 8:30 if that's cool with you."

"Works for me," I say before giving him a subtle smile to hide my true excitement.

At 8:25 in the morning, I hear Joey's SUV pull into the driveway. I look at myself in the mirror one last time. I'm wearing my favorite pink dress and a pair of Steve Madden boots. I hope I'm not overdressed for a casual coffee date, but at least I feel confident in what I'm wearing as I'm about to meet two girls I don't know and invite them to join a coven with me.

A moment later, I hear a faint knock on the door. I take a final breath and shut off the light before heading downstairs. When I open the front door, Joey is standing there with his hands behind his back.

"Hey," I say. "Why are you standing like that?"

He grins from ear to ear. "Okay, it's super cheesy, but these are for you."

"You brought me flowers?" I ask.

He looks away, rubbing the back of his neck. "Uh, well, yeah. My neighbor had these flower, er, plant things in her yard, so I picked a couple and popped them in a mason jar for you. Ms. Sanderson said they're called butterfly bushes. I don't know. I guess it's kind of a silly gesture, but their pink hue reminded me of your color magic."

"Oh, wow. That's super sweet of you. Thank you," I say, taking the jar to set it on the entryway table. *How come the most romantic gesture a guy has ever done for me has to come from a guy who has a fucking girlfriend?*

"Nah, it's no big deal. Just something friends do."

Oof. There it is—the gut punch. I've got to quit thinking about this guy like this. Shit, maybe I need to get back on a dating app here and find someone, so I can really just be friends with Joey without wanting him like I do.

"Right. Well, thank you again," I say. "You ready?"

"Yup, let's do this," he says as he walks to the passenger side of his SUV to open up my door for me.

When he does, I tease him, "Do you do this for all your friends?"

"Nah, only the extra-special ones," he says with a smile.

Butterflies begin to take flight in my stomach, and I wonder if there is something about that damn butterfly bush that's going to have this extra effect on me.

I hop in and see that he's listening to a country music playlist. I laugh because I've always loved country music, but Luna would rather one-up van Gogh and cut both her ears off before listening to it.

When Joey gets in the driver's seat, he notices me jamming out to it already.

"Fan of Luke Bryan?"

"Mm-hmm. It comes off as a surprise to a lot of people, but I do love country music."

He flashes me a smile. "Yeah, I can relate. But, it's just so damn good and catchy. I love that there are so many stories told within the songs too."

"Yes, I couldn't agree more." The song then switches to "Take Me Home, Country Roads" by John Denver, and we both start belting out the lyrics at the top of our lungs. We sing the whole ride over until Joey pulls into a parking spot at the Crunchy Bean.

It's a bigger place than I expected, but when we walk in, it still has a cozy vibe to it. Joey touches my shoulder and whispers in my ear, "They're over there. Follow me." A tingle shoots up my spine from the feeling of him so close to me.

We walk over to a couple seated at a booth by the window.

The guy looks over at me. His chocolate eyes match Joey's but his hair is a fiery red in comparison with Joey's soft brown. They both have the same longer-shaped nose too. I give a little wave since I've been staring a bit long. He waves back and the natural strawberry-blond-haired girl turns around to look at me. Her hazel eyes meet mine, and I offer a smile. She gives a half smile back, and I feel a standoffish vibe from her.

Joey stands near the side of the booth and waves his hands for me to scooch in first. When we both are seated, Artie gives a friendly "Hi there, Zara. I've heard so much about you."

"Have you?" I ask as my face flushes.

"Indeed. Joseph here thinks very highly of you for taking on Granny Lizzie's old shop. He says you and your sister are really making it into something special."

"Well, thank you," I say, glancing over to Joey and smiling. I turn my attention back to Artie and Allegra. "You both should totally come by and check it out sometime. We're actually having a grand reopening two weeks from today. We'd love to see you guys there."

"Yeah, that sounds great," Artie says. My eyes shift to Allegra, who hasn't said a single word since we've sat down. I take in her features for a moment, noticing how absolutely gorgeous she is. She catches me staring and gives me the stink eye. Is she a bitch or something? I cannot read her at all. Her aura is giving off positive, calm vibes and energy, but she has some major walls up.

"Allegra, what do you do for work?" I ask, hoping to squeeze out more than a single word from her.

"I model."

Well, shit. That didn't go very well. I guess two words is better than one.

"Oh, how lovely," I say. "Artie, what about you?"

He cringes. "In construction with Joseph. We work together. And by the way, only Joseph calls me Artie. Just to piss me off. I actually go by Arthur."

"What? Really? I'm so sorry. I had no idea." I elbow Joey in the side playfully and he gives a pathetic pouty face. I won't admit how damn adorable it is. "Wait—do you go by Joseph and I've been calling you Joey the whole time?"

He and Arthur both belly laugh in unison. I look at Allegra, who maintains her RBF. Holy Mother, this girl won't budge.

"Nah, I do go by Joey. That's why I mess with him and call him Artie. I personally think Joey and Artie are much cooler names. Right?" He looks at Allegra. She gives another half smile. Better than nothing, I guess.

"Want me to go grab us some coffees?" Joey asks me before getting up out of the booth.

"Yeah, I'll come with you," I say, jumping up behind him. I am not prepared to be alone with these people.

He smirks and tilts his head, holding out his hand for me as I stand. We accidentally hold hands for a second before I quickly pull away. *This is not good, girl. Get it together.*

"Sorry about that," he says. I brush it off and get in the line. We order our coffees and some pastries before making our way back over to Arthur and Allegra. Fueled by some caffeine, I decide to rip off the Band-Aid.

"So, Joey and I found something out recently about all of our families and ancestors." I then take a sip of my coffee, hoping that Joey will do some of the talking.

He takes the reins and fills them in on our latest discovery while the two of them listen, wide-eyed.

"And all of this is real? You're not bullshitting us, right?" Arthur asks.

"Nope, no BS from us," I offer before adding, "In fact, it's so real that we'd love to invite you to join our coven, Allegra."

She perks up and sets her coffee cup down on the table. "Wait, me? Really?"

"Really. My sister and I just moved here, and we're honoring our grandmother's wishes and trying to keep her legacy. It would mean the world to us to have you."

And for the very first time, she grins from ear to ear.

"Okay, as long as you're sure I'm invited, then count me in."

Joey holds his hand up for a high five, and I'm not sure what I'm more excited about at the moment.

The ride to Evanora's house feels short since we had another jam sesh the entire time. When we pull up into her gravel driveway, I take a quick inventory of our surroundings. We're in a mobile home community and a lot of people are sitting outside staring at us. I hope we have the right place.

"You sure this is it?" I ask Joey.

"Seventy-eight Chestnut. How are you feeling about this one?"

I exhale. "I'm worried that because she has no connections to any of you she's going to react negatively."

Joey looks at me, my silhouette reflected in his dark brown eyes.

"Be yourself. You're going to do great. She's going to trust you," he reassures. "And if she doesn't, you've got the journal, right?"

I unzip the top of my backpack to ensure the journal is still there. I nod and let out a deep breath.

"You've got this, Zar. And remember, I'm right here with you." The butterflies are back in town, but I can't let this distract me.

I thank him and we walk up to Evanora's house. Joey gives a gentle knock on the door. No one answers.

I can feel that someone is there, so I nod for him to knock again. He does, and this time, a young brunette girl with big brown doe eyes opens the door. She looks to be in her early twenties.

"Can I help you?" she asks.

"Hi," I say. "I'm Zara, and this is Joey." He gives a wave.

"Okay, hi. What do you guys want?" Her tone is laden with fear.

"Nothing bad. We come in peace. We actually found out some information about a distant relative of yours, a Lydia Fata. Your last name is Fata, right?"

She nods. "Well, I'm adopted but yes, that's me. My parents died when I was young so I don't know anything about my original family. I just decided to keep my family name."

I pull out the journal to show her as proof. She glances at it briefly before opening the door all the way and letting us in. We follow her to a seating area, but it's covered with stuff. It's not full-blown hoarding, but pretty darn close. I move some stuff to make room to sit and Joey does the same.

"What other info do you have?"

I give her a smile, and tell her that it might sound a bit overwhelming at first, but she says nothing scares her anymore.

"Lydia Fata was actually in a witch's coven with one of my and my sister Luna's relatives. We're witches too, and we're looking to form our own coven with some of the descendants. You're still local and we think it'd be great to have you join us."

"Witches, huh?" she remarks in disbelief. "I'm not sure if I believe in that kind of thing. Sorry, I think you have the wrong girl."

I look at Joey for a second and he gives me an encouraging nod. Before my eyes return to Evanora, I notice a china cabinet filled with crystals.

"I understand your hesitation. It's a lot to take in. But are those your crystals?"

Evanora nods. "Oh yes, I collect them. I've always been drawn to their beauty and the way they make me feel."

I smile at her and she smiles back. "Well, those are things we believe in. The healing power and magic of crystals. So I definitely think we have the right girl."

She shifts uncomfortably before standing. "I think it's time for you guys to go. Thanks for stopping by. I'm sorry I don't have more information for you."

Joey tilts his head toward the door, and I cave. Evanora holds the door open for us, but before I leave, I turn to her one more time. I search my bag for one of our shop's business cards and a flier for the grand reopening.

"Even if you're not interested in joining our coven, my sister and I would love to get to know you more. We're new in town and could really use some new friends. So, if you're down for two new friends, come check out the reopening of our grandmother's apothecary."

Evanora stares at the card and flier. "Wait—Enchanted Elixirs. I love that place. Is Granny Lizzie your grandmother?"

"Yeah, she is. Did you know her?"

"Not super well, but she was always the sweetest when I went into the shop. Especially if I was on the hunt for new crystals." She pauses and looks over to her collection.

"I'm not surprised. Our gran was truly one of a kind." I take a step out the door that she's still holding open. I spot Joey waiting for me by the car. "Well, it was so nice to meet you," I say. "Hope to see you at the grand reopening."

She smiles. "I'll definitely be there."

"Sounds good," I say.

And right as I'm about to turn around, her big brown eyes look at me and she says, "And you know what? Count me in on the coven too. Give me the details at the shop. See you then."

"See you then, Evanora," I say before giving her a final wave and flashing Joey the biggest smile on my way over to the passenger side.

SIX

It's been a lot of work, but after a couple weeks, we're finally ready for the grand reopening of Enchanted Elixirs. The shop is spruced up, painted, fixed, and revamped. We got the sign redone, and it now hangs proudly with a gorgeous and alluring font for everyone to see. The inside is a perfect combination of mystical and slightly ominous. We really wanted a whole new vibe with this place, and I think it's safe to say we accomplished it. The walls are now a dark charcoal gray, almost black. The lighting is still low and intimate, but we updated the fixtures and the shelves are still full of products, but it doesn't feel so crowded and overwhelming. We purged a lot of what Gran had before. We also added a little lobby area up front with dark antique furniture. Honestly, it's just as much for us as it is for our customers. When it's slow, it'll be a cozy place to relax.

I do a final walk-through to make sure everything is in its correct place. It's unnecessary considering I myself have already done this three times, Zara twice, and Gwyn a whopping five. The woman is organized and just as motivated to make this place a success as we are. She was even able to get press here for the event. I'm hoping it will make a big difference and allow us to get our names out there. Not only have we invited our coven, including our potential newest member, Nora, but everyone we know.

We also invited the coven to stay afterward for drinks. And Joey. I can tell that Zara has a thing for him, even though he has a girlfriend. She, of course, would never make a move on someone taken, but his girlfriend isn't the friendliest from what I've heard.

I make my way over to the kitschy section we set up for tourists. I have to admit, it's adorable. We have stones and witch pendulums, along with sage and palo santo, tons of candles, cute little signs and journals, magnets that have witchy phrases on them, and finally, little bottles of "potions" that I made. Honestly, none of them are potent enough to actually do much, but I did put a few ingredients in them that would bolster their purpose. For instance, in a sleeping tonic, I added lavender, melatonin, and GABA. I also made love potions, a luck brew, and one for success. I put them all in cute little vials and bottles, and they each come with their own set of instructions. Overall, I think this section will do really well.

Gwyn has also reached out to all of Gran's old clients who would buy potions and spells from her. There were a few who seemed reluctant, but for the most part they were excited that they were going to be able to purchase them again. We already have a flood of orders for people since the shop was closed for so long, and I'm actually really glad to have projects to work on. I love making potions and performing spells. I'm excited about the apothecary too, obviously, but this is where I really thrive.

I look over at Zara and smile at the flushed and wondrous look on her face. She loves this just as much as I do. We pulled out all the stops on our outfits today, both wanting to look professional and brand ourselves. I'm wearing an all-black pantsuit with a black shirt and vest. The pants are flared at the bottom and I'm wearing some black pumps. I got my nails done the other day with my traditional black-tipped style with little gold stars and moons. My hair is pulled back into a high bun and my makeup is done with a dark smokey eye and a bold wine-colored lip that matches my color magic to a T.

Zara, on the other hand, is my opposite in every way. She opted for a tight-fitting pink dress. Despite the color, it's extremely professional and hugs her curves in all the right places. It comes to just past her knees and she's wearing a pair of nude heels. Her hair is done in long flowing waves that frame her delicate face, with light natural makeup.

"All right, ladies, are we ready?" Gwyn asks.

I take a deep, slightly nervous breath before nodding. Zara seems to be even more anxious than me, and I reach over to squeeze her hand.

"We're ready," I tell her, and the three of us make our way to the front door.

My stomach flips as I see the crowd of people and cameras on the other side of the glass. I do not like being in the spotlight, but I'm pushing through because I know this will be worth it. Zara gives me a squeeze of her own, and I give her a grateful smile. I'm not alone. We're in this together.

We open the doors, making the chime sound above us. I'm immediately assaulted by the cacophony of the crowd. Everyone is cheering and clapping, cameras are flashing. I smile, but it's probably more of a grimace. I rarely smile even for Zara. Smiling for this many strangers and the press is not something that feels natural in the slightest.

There's a big red ribbon in front of us, separating us from the crowd. Zara was insistent that we keep with this tradition of opening a new business. It's harmless, and as cute as she is, I decided to indulge her. We're passed a huge set of scissors and I grab the top half and Zara grabs the bottom half. We open it over the ribbon and pause as the media takes pictures of us. Then, we snip it. As the ribbon falls to the ground, something in the atmosphere of the shop changes. I'm not sure if it's just the excitement surrounding the event, or if maybe I'm imagining it, but something feels different. I push past it as Zara takes the lead.

"Welcome to the new and improved Enchanted Elixirs!" she shouts for the crowd.

They cheer again and we move aside to allow them all to enter. Gwyn moves behind the counter to start checking people out as they're ready, and Zara and I mingle with the crowd, answering questions about merchandise and ingredients.

The press comes around, taking lots of footage of the shop and all of our wares. When they ask us for an interview, I leave it to Zara. She's better with people and more comfortable in front of the camera. She gives me a knowing look but lets me scamper off. Everyone seems to be happy just wandering around, and I make my way behind the counter with Gwyn. As soon as there's a physical barrier between me and the crowd, my anxiety immediately lessens. Not a ton, but enough that I get some relief.

Even though it's packed and Gwyn is busy checking people out, she leans over to whisper to me, "Are you doing okay?"

I'm a little shocked. There's attraction between the two of us, but we don't know each other well. I'm surprised that she caught on to my discomfort.

"Do I not look okay?"

Her brow furrows and I realize how rude that sounded.

"I'm sorry," I say. "I just sometimes struggle being in the spotlight and around a ton of people. Today is just a little much for me."

She gives me a sympathetic smile. "I understand. I get antsy in large crowds too. Do you need to go in the back for a few minutes?"

I touch her lightly on the back, and I notice how her cheeks pink and her eyes heat. "That's sweet of you, but I'll be okay. I just needed a second where I wasn't surrounded by strangers. I feel better now."

She nods but doesn't look convinced. "Okay, well, if you decide you need a break, we can handle it."

"Thanks," I say, moving in closer to her. I'm drawn in by the fire in her gaze. When her eyes dip to my mouth, I almost lean in to kiss her. Before I can, the customer coming up to the register clears their throat. The spell is broken and we pull back from each other.

Embarrassment creeps up my cheeks from not thinking clearly. I can't believe I was about to kiss her in front of the press and our entire new client base on our busiest day. I shake my head at myself. I get out from behind the counter, paste on my friendliest smile, and go talk to our clients.

The day flies by, and my body is absolutely *aching* by the end. I have a headache from the noise, my feet are killing me from the heels, my cheeks are literally throbbing from smiling all day, and I'm also sweating like a witch in a courthouse. But when we finally close up shop, I'm *shocked* when Gwyn tells us how well we did. She's never seen it so busy the entire time she's worked here. In fact, she says that we will already need to put in an order to restock everything. Of course we know that since this was a big event and opening day that we definitely won't be this busy all the time, if ever again, but we at least know that people are interested in the shop and our products.

Hazel, Morgan, and Nora linger, wanting to hang out, but I'm surprised when I see Joey and his girlfriend staying too. I have to admit, she looks like a bitch. Not to mention fake as fuck. She has a look on her face like she smells something foul, but I know she doesn't because our shop smells amazing with all of the natural herbs and oils we have here. Her hair is bleached blond, almost to the point of looking like hay from how damaged it is. I can see her dark brown roots starting to come in, and I wonder how often she has to color it. She has filler in her lips to the point that they look permanently in the duck lips position, and her skin is so tan it has that leathery consistency. And lastly, her fake tits are pressed up so high that I'm surprised she hasn't taken anyone's eyes out yet.

"Do you guys want help cleaning up?" Joey asks. His girlfriend, whose name I won't even bother learning, pouts.

Zara looks like she's about to take him up on the offer, but before she can, Gwyn shoos him out.

"Get the fuck out. No boys allowed."

Zara's face falls, and I almost chime in that he can stay, but then I look at his girlfriend again. She looks much happier at the prospect of leaving, and I really don't want to be stuck with her here. Especially when we're going to be doing coven stuff. I don't trust her with the information. Not that I know what she would even do with it.

"All right, all right," he says, making his way to the door. "The shop looks great, ladies. You did a really wonderful job. Granny Lizzie would be proud."

Zara positively beams. "Thank you so much for coming."

"Yes, thank you," I add.

He gives us a warm smile before taking off, fake-titted bitch in tow behind him.

The rest of the girls stay to help us clean up and to celebrate. I feel bad that during the day we weren't really able to socialize with them at all, but we were so busy that there wasn't time for anything other than "Hi, thanks so much for coming."

Although, Zara told me that while I was busy earlier, Allegra came in to see the shop. She was originally going to stay and hang out, but then she spotted Gwyn, Morgan, and Hazel. Apparently her expression shut down and she said she didn't realize that they were a part of our group. She told her that she didn't know if she would be comfortable being in a coven with them and then took off to "think about it." I'm bummed I didn't have the opportunity to meet her, but I'm hoping she'll come around.

Once we close, I immediately take off my jacket and my heels. "Someone needs to grab the wine right the fuck now. It's an emergency," I tell them dramatically, flopping down on one of our antique-looking plum couches in the lobby.

Gwyn laughs but obliges me. I don't know how she isn't just as exhausted as I am, but she opens the bottles we had in the back for this very moment, pouring us all a large glass. Morgan hands them out, starting with me and Zara. I raise my glass and clink it with my sister's.

"We did it, bitch."

"We sure did, witch," she replies, winking at me.

I laugh but take a greedy drink. Gwyn turns some music on, keeping the volume lowered, and then sits next to me on the couch. I know Zara left the space open for that exact purpose. I see how she looks between us as she tries to play matchmaker. I savor the heat of Gwyn's leg pressing against mine, but do my best to look unaffected.

Everyone gathers around us, and I'm pleased to see that Nora is settling in with everyone. I can tell she's a bit out of her element, but she seems incredibly interested in this new direction. Baby witches are so adorable in their newness.

I take a long drink of my wine before realizing I don't have my phone on me. I left it behind the counter. I roll my eyes at myself before getting up to grab it. Not like I have anyone who would be contacting me. Everyone I know basically is here, but it's a sort of safety blanket.

When I head behind the counter, I feel that same energy I did when we opened the shop. I look around, trying to pinpoint where it's coming from. Now that I'm not overwhelmed by everything, I can focus on it a bit more. It feels almost like...Gran's magic? How is that possible?

I follow it, and find an envelope with her handwriting lying on the desk. I know for a fact that it was not there before because I just came in here before we opened and locked the door behind me. No one could've slipped in to put it here. I run my fingers reverently over her elegant script.

"Lu! What are you doing? Get back out here, sister," Zara yells from the other room.

I leave the envelope exactly where it is for now. We will have time to figure out what this is later, but it needs to be just me and my sister. I don't want the others here for this.

"Coming!" I shout back.

I lock the door behind me again before stopping to grab my phone like I was originally intending.

When I sit back down, Zara is staring at me, and I realize my face must be giving something away. She raises a brow in question, but I give her a subtle shake of my head. *Later*, I tell her with my eyes. She understands what I'm saying in the way only a sister can. She nods back and we continue chatting with everyone.

The more we drink, the closer Gwyn and I get to each other. Our bodies are pressed tight together, and we continue to give each other heated looks. I really want to take her home, but I'm not sure if it's the best idea since she's technically our employee.

"So," Zara drawls now that we've had a few glasses of wine and are feelin' good. "Now that we're open, can we please officially start our own coven? Like for real?"

Her eyes are bright with excitement, and I can tell she likes the idea as much as I do. We didn't like how things were done in our last coven. It felt too big, too fake, and too unwelcome.

"Yes, please!" I say.

Gwyn reaches over and squeezes my knee with just as much enthusiasm as Zara and me. Goosebumps erupt over my skin, but I don't acknowledge them. Instead, I give her a wink before turning back to the group.

"So, what all does this entail?" Nora asks, blushing. "Sorry to ask such an obvious question, but I don't know the first thing about all of this."

"Girl, don't even worry about it. We're all really excited to help you discover your magic," Morgan reassures her.

"Speaking of which, we need to awaken your color magic," I say.

"What's that?" she asks with a nervous lilt.

I hold my hand up and let my wine-purple magic flow from my fingertips. It tidies the space around us quickly and then I gently direct it around all of the girls, encouraging a bit of rejuvenation and reviving energy to all of us. Nora gasps at the feel of my magic intertwining with her.

"It allows you to do a lot of simple magic, and it aids in spells and potions. Each witch usually has their own form or type of magic they excel in, but every witch has the ability to perform color magic once it's awoken inside of them. It's a reflection of who we truly are," I explain.

She looks completely enraptured. "So, you don't know what color your magic will be until it's awakened?"

"Correct," Gwyn says next to me. "And in order for it to awaken we need to perform a ritual."

Nora looks terrified and thrilled all at the same time.

Zara laughs lightheartedly. "Don't worry, babes. It's fun. And not painful or stressful in the least."

Zara is so good at reassuring people. She's always been such a people person. I would say I wish I had more of that quality in me, but honestly, I fuckin' hate people most of the time.

Nora nods. "Okay. Let's do it."

"Well, we can't quite yet. The ritual has to be performed under a full moon, so we'll need to wait a week. We will also need another witch. We need four of you to call each of the elements while Zara and I surround Nora and chant the spell," I say.

She looks a little relieved that we're not about to do it right this second and I chuckle. Newbies.

"Should I text Allegra and see if she'd be willing to come and help us?" Zara asks.

I nod. "That would be perfect." I ignore the other girls groaning in complaint. I know they aren't huge fans of her and say she's not friendly, but a lot of people say that about me too. I have a strange sense that she and I are actually going to have a weird sort of kinship, even though I haven't met her yet. It's also really important to me for us to have all of the descendants of the original coven. And as much as they don't like it, Allegra's part of that as well.

We continue chatting the night away, having more glasses of wine, and it amazes me how comfortable I already am with these women. I've only ever felt this relaxed around my sister, and the fact that I do now with them is astounding. We've hardly spent any time together, but I feel as if I've known them for years.

The hours pass, and the day finally catches up with me. I fight a yawn, and when I look over at Zara, I can see she's having the same difficulty.

"Well, ladies, as much fun as this was, we're absolutely beat. Let's all plan to meet for Nora's awakening ritual and then after we can officially form the coven and decide what all of our roles will be. Hopefully Allegra will be able to attend."

"She says she can make it," Zara confirms.

I nod. "Perfect. The more of us that are here for your awakening, the better! Then, we can do our coven ritual."

Everyone stands, and we close down the shop and I quickly grab Gran's letter before heading home for the night. I already know

I'm going to sleep like the fuckin' dead, but first, we have to read the letter.

"Zara, wait. When we closed the shop I found a letter from Granny Lizzie."

Her tired eyes snap open wide in surprise. "You did? What does it say?"

"I don't know. I haven't read it yet. I wanted to read it with you and not in front of the others."

She nods. "Well, let's see what she has in store for us this time." Her tone is joking, but there's an undercurrent of worry to it. After all, last time we got a letter from her, our entire lives were uprooted.

My dear girls,

I'm so proud of you for taking ownership of the shop and making it new again. I know the apothecary needed much love and updating, and I can only imagine how much work it was to get all of that done. I never had any doubt that you two would manage it with flying colors (literally).

I have spelled multiple letters that will appear to you only in case of certain events, this one included. So keep an eye out for little signs and words of encouragement from me. I know you ladies are going to do wonderful things and I wish I were there to witness everything you accomplish.

Until my next letter,
All my magical love,
Granny Lizzie

A smile is plastered to my face, and when I meet my sister's eyes, I see tears running down her cheeks.

"Granny Lizzie is giving us *such* a gift."

By this point, she's sobbing and I wrap her in my arms, even though I'm inwardly chuckling. She's always such an emotional one. So completely the opposite of me.

"She did," I agree. "It sounds like we're going to have more letters coming."

We break apart and go to bed with our grandmother's praises in our heads.

The next few days are a blur. Zara, Gwyn, and I are all at the shop every spare moment. It's not as busy as opening day, but still much busier than we were expecting. It's a good problem to have.

Needless to say, as the week progresses, it's nice to have things slow down slightly. We're able to take turns going into the shop. When it's my day, I have to admit that it's refreshing to have the place to myself. And as much as I like making money, I do enjoy the quiet and atmosphere of the shop when it's slow.

I take the opportunity to restock some of our potions in our potion and herb room called the Workshop. We talked about making this room more for excess storage, but considering that we're selling potions to the general public, Zara and I needed an adequate space to prepare them.

I get everything going in my cauldron, and add a bit of my color magic so the spoon stirs continuously. When I hear the bell chime at the front of the store, I leave the Workshop and head over to the counter.

A man walks in, and I have to admit that if I wasn't a lesbian, I would definitely find him attractive. He's dressed in all black, his many tattoos on display and his piercings and jewelry glinting in the sunlight. His dark hair falls in a swoop across his prominent brow and he takes in the shop with a curious expression. His full lips, set in a defined jaw, purse slightly, and his green-and-gold-flecked eyes come to rest on me. His stare is intense, and I feel myself bristling.

The hair on the back of my neck rises, but I push past it. "Welcome to Enchanted Elixirs. Can I help you find anything specific?"

He shakes his head. "No, I'm just looking around." His voice is deep and gravelly.

I nod but watch him carefully as he makes his way around the shop, checking out all of our wares. I don't know why, but something about this man sets me on edge.

Eventually, he approaches me at the counter. He gives me a charming smile, and I can tell he's used to getting his way with that grin. I narrow my eyes at him.

"Nice place you have here."

"Thank you. Are you going to buy something?" I try to keep most of the bitchiness from my voice but don't know if I succeed.

His smile remains in place but a coldness enters his expression. "Actually, I was hoping to work here."

His comment takes me so off guard that I don't respond for a few seconds. "You what?"

"I would like to apply for a job."

I don't know why I'm so shocked by the statement, but I am. I wasn't anticipating to already have people inquiring about jobs but especially not this man. He doesn't seem the type to want to work in an apothecary. Not to mention that a few moments ago I was worried about him potentially shoplifting.

"Well, we just opened."

"I know. I found out about the grand reopening online, and it looked like such a unique place that I thought I would come check it out. I really enjoy the atmosphere and think it would be a good fit for me."

"Thank you, but we aren't ready to start hiring yet." I keep my tone friendly but dismissive.

He nods, looking a bit disappointed. "Okay, well, thanks for letting me come in and explore."

I exhale a relieved breath when he leaves. I don't know what the fuck that was, but my heart is racing a bit. I shake off the unnerving sensation and check on my potion.

The full moon is out tonight, and Zara and I are vibrating with excitement. I don't know what it is, but I feel as though everything is about to change.

All of the girls meet us at the shop. It's my first time meeting Allegra, and I can see why the others are wary of her. She has some walls in place, and has an "I don't give a fuck" attitude. She's also incredibly hot. She's not my normal type, but if I wasn't interested in Gwyn, I might have given her another look. That being said, I think once I break through her defenses, she and I will get along swimmingly.

Nora looks nervous, but there's an exhilarated gleam in her eye, and I love that she's seeming ready for tonight. I know that it can be new and scary getting your magic for the first time, but there's also no better feeling in my opinion.

We talked about where would be the best place to do this, and it was tough because Zara and I haven't lived here long, but luckily Gwyn has a little field she uses for rituals that's remote and un-known. She was very adamant that this was *her* field, and we could use it only if we asked her first. It made me chuckle at the time, but I also completely understand. We witches are very territorial, especially regarding our magical spaces. Rituals can be extremely vulnerable, and you need to feel safe in the place you practice.

We all follow Gwyn in her car, and once she stops, we get out and walk to her area. It's off the beaten path, and I can see why no one else has come across it. It's perfect for what we need for tonight. Trees surround us on all sides, but there's a little clearing that allows us to see the sky and pregnant moon clearly.

The mother's moon beams down on me, and I bask in her attention and glow. I've always loved full moons, even if they make me a little crazy.

"So, what do we need to do?" Nora asks.

Everyone looks to me, and I realize I'm going to be guiding this thing. I haven't ever done one of these myself, and my only experience was when my grandmother did this with me and Zara. That being said, I have a photographic memory, and I remember every single second of that night in perfect clarity. Performing it, on the other hand, is a little different and nerve-racking.

I take out the candles that I brought for this very occasion. Four in total. I direct Nora to where I want her, right in the middle of the clearing. Then I hand out each of the candles. The green earth candle I give to Hazel and motion for her to stand to the north. Next, I give the yellow air candle to Morgan and she takes up the eastern spot. Red, fire to Allegra to the south. And finally Gwyn takes the blue water candle to the west.

I go around, lighting each candle surrounding Nora and calling the elements to the circle.

"I invite the cold winds of air.
I welcome the warm light of fire.
I call upon the rushing rivers of water.
And I beckon the great mother earth.
Join us and awaken our new sister."

I can feel each of the elements rush into the space, and it brings a contented smile to my face. Zara and I lock hands, Nora in the middle, surrounded by our enclosed arms. I swear I can feel the Three-Faced Goddess in our circle as well, and Nora gasps when Zara and I start chanting.

Yellow smoke starts billowing out of her as she closes her eyes, head tilted back in a portrait of ecstasy. I can relate.

Minutes later, the flood out of her slows to a trickle before finally stopping. When she opens her eyes and looks at me, they're filled with wonder and amazement.

"That was…" She trails off.

I smile and nod at her. We all know what she's getting at, even if she's unable to voice it.

I disband the elements, thanking them for aiding us before blowing out the candles.

We give Nora a few minutes to collect herself. Getting an influx of magic is incredibly overwhelming at first, even if it's amazing. When she seems composed, we all take a seat in the grass.

"So, how are you guys feeling? Are we ready to make this official?" Zara asks the group.

"Allegra, we'd really like you to join us. Would you be willing to become part of our sisterhood?" I ask.

She looks around, her gaze lingering on the women she's never gotten along with, but I can see the excited gleam in her eyes from doing magic with our group. We click together.

Allegra seems a little hesitant, but nods.

The other women all chime in that they're ready.

I take out my rune-covered bowl with my special knife. I try not to think about the fact that the last time I used these it was to change Chad into a cat.

I pour my favorite red wine into the bowl before slicing my finger open, letting my blood mix with the wine. I pass it to my sister and she does the same, although I chuckle when she hisses in a sharp breath. She's never been able to handle pain well.

All the others follow suit, and when the cup is back in my hands, I hold it up in a toast to our coven, the Three-Faced Goddess, and the moon. I take a healthy swig, tasting the tang of the blood with the booze. When I pass it to Zara, I release my color magic into the center of our circle. Zara follows with her pink magic, Nora with her yellow, Morgan with her blue, Hazel with her green, Allegra with her red, and finally Gwyn with her dark purple, almost black magic. It all coalesces into a rainbow of magic, and the sight is something truly spectacular to behold.

"Blessed be," I say.

"Blessed be," they all repeat in unison.

I feel something snap into place between us all as the color magic explodes around us.

"And so, the Coven of the Crescent Moon is formed." My words echo throughout the clearing.

seven

Zara

After Luna's words, we head back to the apothecary. Something is pulling us to the Moon Room. A letter rests atop the former coven's journal.

Girls,

Congratulations on forming your own coven! In doing so, the rest of the journal's secrets will now be revealed. Please take from it what you desire.

So proud of you two.

All my magical love,

Granny Lizzie

After I read Gran's words aloud, the other girls form a circle around me as I open the journal. I flip it open to the first page to see the list of the coven members remains. I turn to the second page where each member and their color of magic are listed together.

"They had such similar colors to us," Morgan says after I read them to the group.

I flip to the next page as the other girls nod in agreement. At the top of the page, the words *Moon Temple Coven Retreat* are written. Underneath the text, there is unfamiliar handwriting. I skim it until it's revealed that it was a journal entry from one of the three Stonecroft sisters, Mary. The next two are from the other sisters, Winnie and Sarah. I continue to flip through the rest of the coven's journal entries all about their retreat.

"So, it appears that they went on a retreat together to form a stronger bond as a coven. And, there's mention of some kind of sacred bowl they used to put their color magic in, which reveals the true power they each held." I look up from the journal to see the excited faces of my coven sisters around me.

"Do you mean that bowl over there?" Hazel asks, pointing to a bowl resting on the table across from us. We all exchange glances, and Allegra picks it up and examines it. "Seems like an ordinary bowl to me."

Luna snatches it out of her hands. "I bet it's supposed to appear that way, but that's where the magic comes in."

"Yeah, let's think of it as our own Sorting Hat, but a plain fucking bowl," Gwyn deadpans. We all laugh. She really is great to have around.

"So, what should we do with it?" Nora asks, looking to me and Luna.

An idea pops into my mind and Lu looks at me. "Are you thinking what I'm thinking?"

"For the first time in a while, I think so," I say with a sly smile. "Our own retreat?"

"Yes, bitches," Gwyn interjects. "I've been wanting this to happen."

Luna places both her hands on her hips, and I can tell she's already planning the whole thing. "Let's do it!"

"My brother gets married next week though, so can we do it after that?" Allegra asks.

"Yeah, and I need to let work know at least two weeks ahead of time, so could it be in a couple of weeks?" Hazel requests.

Luna and I nod at each other. "Yeah, that's totally doable. It gives us time to think about the logistics too. What do you all think? A coven retreat in a few weeks?"

Everyone nods in agreement.

"Well, girls, I'd say our first official meeting was a success," I say to everyone.

"It seriously was a bomb-ass coven meeting. I'm so excited for what's to come," Luna adds.

Everyone looks around at each other unsure of what to do next, until Gwyn pipes up. "Okay, so how do we formally end this shit anyway?"

Luna looks at me, and when I feel the pressure, I shout, "Moon Sisters, out!"

The coven repeats, "Moon Sisters, out!" and we all giggle and make our exit.

When we reach the top of the stairs and close the hidden passageway, Gwyn whispers to me and Luna, "Hey, girls, can we chat in private for a minute?"

We both recognize the seriousness of her tone and agree. "Let's go chat in the Workshop," I offer.

"Could we go back down to the Moon Room instead?" she asks.

We nod. Luna says, "Let me first make sure the shop door is locked since it's after hours."

"Good call," Gwyn says.

When Luna returns, the three of us head downstairs and take a seat at the table. Luna and I both look at Gwyn.

"Okay, girls. There is something I've been meaning to tell you about Granny Lizzie. I've been trying to figure out how to, but I think I just need to say it."

A bead of sweat forms on my forehead. Luna's eyes widen and focus on Gwyn, and I can feel my heart rate increase.

"What's going on? Is it something bad?" I ask.

Gwyn shakes her head. "No, nothing bad."

"Okay, phew. You're really scaring me," I admit.

"Me too," Luna says.

Gwyn's voice stays quiet when she says, "Your grandmother was actually over 350 years old."

"What? Excuse me? That's impossible. Right?" I look over to Luna.

"You know this for sure? She looked so young," she says.

Gwyn nods. "It's true. I would see her often worry about making sure her aging spell was up-to-date. You see, she would've looked really young had she not been making herself appear older with magic. It was how she was never discovered."

"But how? How could she be so old?" I ask, feeling so confused.

"I don't know the specifics. All I know is that she had a longevity spell on her. With her using the 'aging' spell on herself she was able to make it seem like she was the age she was supposed to be. I think when it would get to the point where people would start asking questions she would fake her own death, change her first name, and reverse the aging spell so she appeared young again, acting like she was a relative of her older self."

I stare at Gwyn, speechless. Luna's eyes narrow. "So, she just lived all this time until recently?"

"Yeah, it's heartbreaking, but I know she really wanted to go. She lived for so long that it was the equivalent of many lives, and the one with your mom bringing you two girls into the world was her favorite. She'd talk about it all the time."

"Do you know anything about our grandfather? All we know is that he died when our mom was young," Luna says.

Gwyn shrugs. "I only know the same thing. She said she was heartbroken to lose him—George, I believe was his name. He died in a car accident, but I got the feeling from her that she believed someone staged it. Back then, they didn't really take the time to look into it further, so she accepted it and had to move on with finally raising a daughter."

"So our mom was her only child?" I ask.

"Yeah, that's how she made it sound," Gwyn says.

Luna exhales loudly and scoffs. "Well, what a fucking disappointment that must've been for her. Our mom was never kind to her and abandoned her here."

"Oh, that's one more thing she told me. The longevity spell kept her in Salem. That's why when your mom took you girls away, she wasn't able to come and visit. And she was always fearful of new technology like airplanes and shit anyway."

"I can't believe we're just now hearing about this. How could Mom not tell us?" A tear wells up in the corner of my eye.

"To be honest, I don't think your mom knew either. I only know because my ancestor Ruth was your grandmother's best friend. She told her when the spell was put on her to begin with, and the secret has been passed down in my family ever since. Rue never wanted her to feel alone. My family has been close with Lizzie ever since."

"Oh, that makes so much sense," I admit.

"So, she lived all that time and was stuck in one place for so long, I don't blame her for finally wanting to be done with it all. I can't even fathom how lonely and frustrating that would be." Luna lets out a deep sigh.

"For real," I add.

Luna leans in and flashes Gwyn a smile. "Thank you for sharing that with us. It means a lot."

"Any other deets you can fill us in on about our grandmother?" I ask.

Gwyn shakes her head. "That's it, girls. Feels really fucking good that you both know now since I was feeling a bit awkward knowing something about your granny that you guys didn't."

Luna nods and stands to her feet. Gwyn and I do the same.

"Yeah, thank you," I say. "Oh, and before I forget. I wanted to ask what you both thought of me bringing Binxi into the shop some days with me."

"Really?" Luna's left eyebrow arches.

"Yeah, it gets a little lonely sometimes, and I'd love to have some company."

"Binxi is your cat, right?" Gwyn clarifies.

"Mm-hmm," I answer. Gwyn gives Luna a look I can't quite place, but then she quickly responds with "That's fine with me."

Luna agrees.

"Great, it's settled. Thanks, guys."

We all smile and make our way back up the stairwell into the shop.

"Do you need us to do anything tonight in preparation for you opening tomorrow, Zar?" Luna asks me.

I glance around to make sure everything is in order. Things are organized, but I've been getting really creepy vibes or seeing things lately, so I can't say I love working alone in the shop. But, I know the two of them would blow it off, especially because if I do notice something or someone in my peripheral vision, the minute I turn my head, no one is actually there. Maybe I just need more sleep.

"I'm all set, thanks," I say, hoping they can't sense the small note of fear in my voice. "Let's go home."

"Sounds good," my sister says.

Gwyn flashes me a quick wave. "See ya, ladies. Can't wait to meet Binxi and have him here with us in the shop some days. He might be a real hit with the customers too."

"Absolutely," I say before giving her a wave goodbye.

The next day, I head into the shop for my shift alone. Well, with the exception of Binxi. He roams the floor, and I also brought in a little kitty house for him to hang out in.

As I unlock the door, I notice an elderly couple approaching. I open the door for them and smile. "Welcome to Enchanted Elixirs," I say.

"Thank you," the gentleman replies. His hand guides the woman at her back, and I can't help but think about how sweet it would be to have a love like that one day.

I let them wander around the shop for a few moments before asking, "Anything specific I can help you two find?"

"We're fine, deary," the woman responds.

I nod. "Okay, well, please let me know if there is anything you need."

The two of them start discussing potions to improve their life in the bedroom and I take that as my cue to not intrude unless they ask. Which, hopefully, they don't.

I make my way over to the counter to wait for them to check out when the door opens. A man enters and my breath hitches when I see him. He has to be the most drop-dead gorgeous human I've ever laid eyes upon. His jawline is perfectly defined, and he's dressed in all black to match his hair—a little on the longer side and slicked back but still framing his beautiful face. He steps closer and flashes me the brightest smile. Two tiny dimples appear, making his first-impression bad-boy look fade away. My cheeks redden as he continues to smile at me, piercing me with his green eyes.

"Hello," he says. His voice deep and smooth.

I watch in horror as my hand does its usual awkward wave thing whenever I'm attracted to someone. "Hi," I say, my voice quivering. "How can I help you?"

"How *can* you help me?" he says, running his fingers through his hair, exposing his sleeve of tattoos. I don't even know what they are, but they're just sexy as fuck. A drop of saliva hits my lower lip and I suck it back in. *What the hell? Am I drooling?* I exhale slowly and try to regain my composure.

The older couple makes their way up to the counter. "Miss, I believe we're all set here," the wife says sweetly.

Thank the Mother for the much-needed distraction. I slowly turn my gaze from the tall, dark, and handsome man who just walked in the door, focusing solely on the sweet couple in front of me. Or, at the very least, trying to.

After I bag up the couple of items they purchased and teach them how to use the fancy new credit card machine we have, I thank them and they exit the shop. Leaving me with just the gorgeous dude. Alone.

I notice him over by the potions. I try not to stare, but it's hard not to. *Should I go ask him what he really does need help with? What is he even doing here?*

Before I can internally debate for too long, the door opens and a cute young strawberry blonde enters. I give her a kind smile, and she returns it and makes her way around the shop. I let her wander for a few moments before approaching her.

"Are you finding everything okay?"

"I'm just checking out what you have here."

"Okay, well, let me know if you need any help."

I'm about to walk away when she stops me. "Actually, there is something I need. Do you happen to have mugwort?"

"Of course." I lead her over to where it's located.

"Oh, this is perfect," she says, picking some up. "This is just what I was looking for. I've been trying to make this potion for so long, but I couldn't find any to save my life. I thought about buying some online, but you never know what you're going to get."

I nod emphatically. "I know exactly what you mean. I hope you don't mind me asking, but I'm assuming you practice magic?"

She nods. "I'm not in a coven or anything, but I do enjoy doing it on my own."

I give her a kind smile as she turns to face me. My eyes immediately lock on to the mark on her eyebrow. While I try not to stare, I can't help it. It's shaped like a—

"Looks just like a crescent moon, doesn't it?" she says.

I chuckle and cup my mouth with my hand. "I'm so embarrassed. I'm sorry for staring, but yes, it looks *exactly* like a crescent moon."

"Yeah, everyone does. It honestly doesn't bother me. I love talking about it." Her bubbly personality has captured my attention that for a split second, I forget Gorgeous Bad Boy is still wandering around the shop.

My eyes shift to him, and I catch him staring at me. He smiles and gives a slight nod, so I give him the same. All these little distractions are sure helping me.

"Well, is there anything else you need?"

"I'm also hoping to pick up a gift for a friend. Do you have anything here that would make a good present?"

I nod, guiding her over to the self-love boxes. I help her pick one out that includes her friend's favorite scented candle and crystal. "And the herbs in there are for sure going to make her feel so damn good about herself," I explain while I finish checking her out. "The angelica creates harmony and courage, beech for happiness, and finally chamomile for love and stress relief."

"All set," I say, handing her the box.

"Thanks so much. It was fabulous to meet you..."

"Zara," I supply. Binxi jumps up on the counter then. "And this rascal is Binxi."

She lets out a surprised squeak, chuckling before giving him a scratch on his head. "Well, nice to meet you, Zara and Binxi. I'm Ariadne."

I smile. "You too, Ariadne. Hope to see you back in the shop again soon."

She begins walking away, but says, "You definitely will. This crescent moon witch shall return."

I giggle at her comment, glad someone else is just as awkward as I am, before turning my head back to where the sexy man was. He is no longer standing by the lotions and oils, so I search the room for him, checking the hidden passageway entrance. He's standing next to it, and even though he must sense I'm there, he doesn't make eye contact with me. For a brief moment, I swear he's staring right at the crescent moon that's used to open the passageway.

"So, seriously, how can I help you?" I ask, feeling bolder than I had before. He pops his hands into his pockets and makes his way closer to me.

My eyes instantly fall to his mouth with its well-defined Cupid's bow.

"I'm Viktor, but you can call me Vik," he says, reaching his hand out for a…handshake? For some reason, this doesn't suit him, but I go ahead and shake his hand. It's soft, but so damn cold.

"Zara," I respond and pull my hand away slowly.

"Your name is as gorgeous as you are, Zara," he says, annunciating my name so it sounds like the sexiest name a person could have.

Pink finds its way to my cheeks, and I can't help but release a tiny gasp.

"Thank you," I say.

He nods. "My pleasure." Vik shifts his body, feet pointed toward me. "I actually came by because I'm new in town. Just moved from Rhode Island. And this shop just felt really homey and inviting. I felt compelled to come in here."

"Thank you," I say again.

His pierced eyebrow rises. "Are you going to keep thanking me for everything I say?"

I laugh. "Ha, oops. Sorry."

"I don't mind it," he says, his eyes twinkling. "I'd love it if I had someone to show me around. Do you know of anyone who might be interested in doing so?"

My body tingles at the idea of showing him around, and maybe getting to know him better. I haven't slept with anyone since Chad, and as much as I like Joey, he's got Tiffany so there's no chance there. "I'd absolutely love to. I'm off in about five hours when my sister takes over if you want to meet up and I can show you around."

"Oh?" he asks. I watch as the left side of his mouth turns upward, forming a half smile. Between his crooked smile and those sexy green eyes sparkling with tiny golden flecks staring at me has my heart racing and my cheeks burning. *Good Goddess, he is so damn fine.*

"Yeah, I'm happy to give you whatever you need." *Me. My body. My soul.*

"Mmm," he says. "It sounds to me like you're a bit of a giver, aren't you?"

Well, fuck me. I'm so turned on by this man, I'd give him anything he wanted right here, right now. I nod and release a tiny whimper.

He inches closer to me, and my breathing slows. Out of the corner of my eye, I notice what looks like someone staring at me through the window. My eyes quickly shift, but no one is there. I glance back at Vik, who appears to be even closer than I remember. His eyes dart to my lips, and I want nothing more than for him to pull my face to his and kiss me until I can't stand it.

Instead, he says, "I actually can't today. I've really got to find myself a job as soon as possible."

"Oh, what kind of job are you looking for?" I ask.

"At this point, anything will suffice. I am getting fairly desperate." He looks around the shop and then his eyes meet mine again. My knees instantly go weak.

"What if you work with me?" I ask. "Uh—I mean, work here. At the shop."

His eyes narrow as though he's determining whether I'm joking or not. "Really? Are you sure about that?"

"Absolutely. My sister and I just spruced up the place a bit, and I think it'd be great to have a man's perspective in here with us. Plus, I just know she'll love you." I shift my body, hoping I didn't make him feel uncomfortable or pressured. "If you want to, of course."

"I don't know if I could impose like that. But, I will tell you I'm very interested in magic, so this shop seems like a great fit."

"Oh hell yes, you'll fit right in. You should definitely consider it," I say and flash him a big smile.

Vik moves slightly to the right when I notice a woman staring at me through the window behind him. She has red hair and piercing green eyes. I wonder if that's who I saw a second ago. This time, she really is there, staring at me, seemingly taking in my features. A prickle shoots down my spine. Something about her presence chills me. I wonder if she's the reason I've been feeling watched lately.

"Well, if you insist..." he says, directing my focus back to him.

"Definitely. This is going to be so great," I say, hoping Luna truly feels the same way I do.

Vik takes my hand in his. "Thank you, Zara. You have no idea how much this means to me."

"I'm so happy to help," I say, giving him a big smile.

He smiles back, and my whole body trembles. It's as though I'm about to melt into a puddle on the floor at any second.

"So then, now that I've got a new job, are we still on for tonight?" he asks.

I nod enthusiastically.

"Can't wait. I'm excited to see what trouble we'll get into," he says with a wink.

"Me too," I say, knowing damn well the last thing I need right now is trouble.

EIGHT

I walk into the shop, ready to take over for my sister, when I see something I was not expecting.

"Luna, meet our newest employee! This is Vik. I just hired him this morning."

I gape at my sister and the handsome man who's standing behind the counter with her. I recognize him as the same man who came into the shop and asked me for a job. The fact that Zara hired him without asking me about it absolutely baffles me. And boils the fuck out of my blood.

Zara sees the look in my eyes and her face falls. I hate to be the one to make her wear that expression, but it's not fair of her to make this decision without me.

"Zara, can we talk in private?"

She nods before looking back at the man. "Viktor, I'm so sorry, but can you excuse us for a moment?"

He nods, returning to whatever work Zara had him doing before I walked in.

Zara and I make our way to the Workshop and I close the door firmly before turning to her. "How the hell could you make this decision without me? We agreed that all choices about the business would be made *together*. We *both* own this business. I have every right to have a say in the people that work here, Zara." I try to keep my voice even, but I don't succeed.

Her face falls and I can tell she's on the verge of tears. "Luna, I'm sorry. I didn't think. He came in and we started chatting about how he's new in town and doesn't have a job yet. Plus, he's really interested in the occult. I thought he would be the perfect fit. Especially since we're going on that coven retreat soon. We need someone to watch the shop."

I take deep breaths in through my nose. She has a point there, but I don't want to admit it.

"Plus, he's real fuckin' pretty," I remark.

She blushes. "That has nothing to do with it, Luna."

But the fact that she's avoiding eye contact tells me that I hit the nail right on the head. I decide to cut her a break. Even though I hate that she doesn't think things through properly. Especially when a pretty man is involved. Her kitty tends to take the reins in that case.

"Well, did you at least look at his résumé and interview him and do all of the things before you just hired him?"

"Of course I did. And I'm going to teach him. You won't have to do anything. I'll train him and everything."

I sigh heavily. I still don't like it, and I don't trust him, but I can tend to take a while to warm up to people.

"Fine," I draw the word out dramatically.

She claps excitedly before rushing over and giving me a hug. I half-heartedly return it before shoving her away from me. "I better go meet him officially, then, huh?"

She nods. "I think you'll really like him."

I almost scoff. Zara thinks that about everyone. I don't correct her though.

We go back out to the front and now that my temper isn't roiling like an angry sea, I realize she's having him restock.

"Luna, I'd like you to meet Viktor, our newest employee. He just moved here from Rhode Island."

I walk up to him and hold out my hand like a polite person, even though I'm anything but. "Nice to officially meet you, Viktor."

He nods and grips my hand firmly. "Likewise."

I grind my teeth, but at the same time I do get it. Our last interaction wasn't great considering I basically asked him if he was planning on stealing something from our shop and then denied him a job when he asked nicely. Not to mention he probably heard me rip into Zara about hiring him not five minutes ago.

"So, how are you liking our shop so far?" I attempt to put a bit more effort in, giving him a smile, though I know it doesn't look sincere.

"Yes, it's beautiful. I'm excited to learn more about all things magical." He gives Zara a sexy smirk. "So, I heard you all are going on a little retreat with some of your friends?"

I nod. "We aren't sure when yet exactly, but now that you're here we should be able to go after you're fully trained and comfortable. We're thinking in about three weeks or so."

"I'm glad I can be of service. Have you decided where you're going yet?"

"Not yet!" Zara pipes in a little too enthusiastically. I fight a chuckle. She always gets like this with hot guys. "Do you have any recommendations?"

I roll my eyes at her even though no one is looking at me. She already knows he just moved here, like us.

"No, unfortunately I haven't been here long enough yet."

She giggles. "Oh, of course. I forgot."

I leave them to their flirting and go into the Workshop. Watching other people, especially my sister, making googly eyes at each other makes me want to gag.

I work on my current potions, restocking the ones for the shop before turning my attention to the one I need to make for our retreat. It takes longer than my usual concoctions and is also more difficult.

I open the journal, turning to the page with the ingredients. Yowza. So many. Also, there are a few that are going to have to sit in a salt bath marinade under the moon for a week or two. And we wanted to use this on our retreat. It looks like we'll have to wait to schedule it until we know the potion is going to be ready.

As I'm looking through our pantry to see what we have and what we need to buy, Gwyn comes in. My heart picks up slightly at her proximity, and I give her a smile that's probably more sultry than I'm intending. I can't help it. I'm so into this witch. She returns it, looking just as attracted to me.

Lately, I've been feeling like this thing between us is inevitable. I've been trying to keep her at somewhat of a distance so I don't potentially fuck things up with our best employee, but from what I can tell, we're both so interested in each other, there's no avoiding it. Not with us seeing each other regularly.

"What are you working on?" she asks, her voice low.

"I'm trying to start on this potion that we'll need for our little power thingy."

"Power thingy?" she questions, laughter coating her words.

"My brain isn't braining right now, but you know what I mean."

She comes closer. "I think it's cute."

My breath catches at how close we are to each other now, as though we're being drawn together like magnets. Her eyes dip to my lips. My tongue darts out to wet them, and her gaze latches on to the movement.

"You think I'm cute?" I whisper. I meant to have a teasing tone to my voice, but instead, all that coats my words is *want*.

"You know I do." She's suddenly so serious.

The fact that she just admitted to the attraction between us throws reason completely out the window. Without another thought, I surge forward and capture her lips with mine.

Her mouth is soft, pillowy, and pliant underneath mine and she melts into me. My arms come around her, pulling her as close as I can. Our heights are similar, making our breasts press firmly together, and when I push my tongue into her mouth, her nipples pebble in excitement against me. I moan at the feel of it, and in response, she tangles her hands in my hair.

The kiss becomes more heated as we fight for dominance. She pushes me against the workstation and bottles rattle behind us, but I don't care. All I can think about is the fact that this woman is finally in my arms, right where I want her, kissing even better than I've been imagining.

I scoot back and up, sitting my ass on the counter space so I can get her in between my legs. She follows me back, and I wrap my legs around her waist, pressing us even closer than before.

In our excitement, one of the bottles clatters to the ground, shattering. I'm ready to ignore it, but then I hear my sister's voice cutting through my haze of lust.

"Is everything okay back there?"

I break away from Gwyn. "Fuck," I whisper. "Yeah, everything's fine. Just dropped a vial," I yell out.

Gwyn is still in front of me, but the moment has passed. Reality crashes back in around us. She takes a step back, giving me a sad smile. I give her an equally sad nod and watch as she walks out of the room as quietly as she entered.

The potion is *finally* ready. I couldn't be more relieved. As far as I can tell, it looks as it should. I've never made it before, but from the descriptions in the journal, it's correct. Only one way to find out.

Gwyn knows of the perfect location, apparently. There's a cabin that she's been to a few times before that's big enough for the whole coven. It's only about an hour away, and there's plenty of nature around for us to feel connected in the traditional witch way. It's no secret that witches love nature, and we will all feel more at ease.

We take two separate cars. Me, Zara, and Allegra in one, along with our faithful sidekick, Binxi. Gwyn, Hazel, Morgan, and Nora in the other. We figured since Allegra was still uncomfortable with the other members of the coven that we would have her ride with us. It gives us the opportunity to learn more about her without the tension the presence of the other girls brings. It's also a chance for Nora to pick the other witches' brains about magic as well. Since her color magic was awakened, she's been finding out anything and everything that she can. I think it's adorable how invested she is in it now, and I'm secretly proud that we were able to introduce her to this part of herself.

In the hour-long drive to the cabin, the three of us chat about everything under the moon. Zara gets along with her, but as I suspected, Allegra and I are meant to be friends. We have the same bitchy attitude that no one understands, as well as the same sarcastic, twisted sense of humor.

We get to the cabin, and I'm delighted when I see there's a lake nearby. I'm a sucker for water, and living in Colorado for so long, I was so deprived of it for years. The fact that this cabin is essentially a lake house thrills me.

We all head in, and Gwyn was right. There are more than enough places for us to sleep. Some girls have to double up, but Morgan and Hazel are essentially best friends and are the first to volunteer. Zara and I also volunteer—we've slept in the same bed more times than I can count. Honestly, it's always been more of a fun, sleepover type thing for us. That being said, we also want the ginormous bed and our own bathroom.

After we get set up in our rooms, we all head down to the kitchen.

"Is everyone hungry?" Hazel asks, unpacking the groceries.

"Are you going to cook for us?" I ask.

"This bitch loves to cook," Morgan chimes in. "It's half the reason I put up with her shit and live with her."

"Yeah, because you are just the perfect angel that anyone would be *honored* to live with," Hazel shoots back.

We all chuckle. Despite their teasing, I can absolutely see how much they love being roommates.

"Soooo, no one answered my question." Hazel looks around at us all expectantly.

"I'm starving. Feed me," I demand.

She giggles but gets to work prepping dinner with Morgan helping her.

"Is it too early for wine?" I ask. Everyone knows I'm the wino in this group.

"It's never too early," Gwyn remarks. Things have been slightly awkward between us ever since the kiss, but we're both attempting to push through it.

I give her an uncomfortable smile, but open a bottle and pour us a glass. We each take a drink before I realize I should ask, "Does anyone else want one?"

Allegra is the only one who takes me up on it, everyone else claiming they want to eat before they start drinking. Amateurs.

Hazel is making fettuccine alfredo with garlic bread and a salad. It smells delicious, and soon my stomach starts rumbling.

"So, are you guys ready for tonight?" Zara asks, excitement in her voice.

Nora once again appears nervous, but everyone seems to be feeling the same way—eager. I don't admit that I'm also slightly nervous too, but for more reasons than just the process of what's to come. I'm anxious about the potion working properly. And admittedly, I also have butterflies in my stomach about Gwyn.

Being this close to her and sleeping in the same house after we've already kissed is going to be rough.

I force my food down through the knots in my stomach. It's delicious, but I always have a hard time eating when I'm anxious.

When night falls and the stars are shining brightly throughout the sky, we head outside. I bring the bowl that our ancestors made specifically for this along with the potion that took longer than any I've made before.

We sit in our classic circle under the brilliant heavens above us. I pour the potion into the bowl before setting it gently in the center. The liquid glows brightly in the starlight, and it reflects the galaxy above, making it seem like an endless universe.

I go first, just in case something went wrong with the potion. I take a deep breath, closing my eyes before extending my hand in front of me and pouring my wine red magic into the bowl. It mixes with the potion, and I watch in amazement as the smoke settles into the liquid, like wine mixing with water.

It takes a few moments for anything to happen. Long enough that I'm positive I fucked something up. But then, an image rises in smoke and moisture. The other girls gasp, and I know they can see it too. I wasn't sure if they would.

A cauldron forms, and I instinctively know that it means my innate magic lies in potions. I think it's going to sink back into the bowl and that will be that, but then another image takes form. Me pouring my blood into my special vessel, and this time I know it's referring to blood magic. The type of magic that my last coven deemed "dark." Then the image sinks back into the bowl and my color fades. I gasp as I feel a surge of power sink into me.

"It worked. I have more power."

The women look at me in amazement, and I gesture for Zara to go next, ready for the others to experience it too, and for us to become a stronger unit.

She goes through the same process, and I'm unsurprised when the image that rises is herbs. She's always been wonderful at growing gardens and making them flourish. It's a beautiful thing actually. She grows the ingredients that I use in our spells. Before it sinks down however, a house comes into view and I smile at that as well. She's always been a house witch, preferring to use magic around the house to make her life more convenient as opposed to using it for anything major.

Nora goes next, and I'm interested in hers. I have no idea what her magic will be since she hasn't had a chance to explore different types yet. Her yellow magic flows into the bowl, and when crystals manifest in the air, it seems fitting. After all, Zara said that she had plenty of stones around her house the first time she went to see her.

Morgan releases her blue magic and I'm shocked to see the cosmos appear. A whole little universe is contained before us. It then changes to a picture of her standing in one place before another version of her appears in another.

"Astral projection," she whispers.

Shit. I've never met anyone who had that skill before. That could be a useful talent to have in our coven. I realize then that Morgan is extremely powerful, and I'm grateful that she's with us.

Hazel's up, and I don't think any of us are surprised by the plants that come to life in the smoke before us. Her green magic screams "earth," and the vibe that she gives off is the exact same.

It's Allegra's turn, and I have a strange feeling about this one. I don't know why, but I get a sense that this will change the dynamic in the group. An image starts to form, and it takes a moment for me to make sense of it, but then it comes into focus and I let out a shocked breath. Sex. That's what I'm seeing. A couple having sex. It makes so much sense why most women don't like her. They're jealous because men are always so attracted to her. But there's no way for her to help it. It's literally part of her innate character.

I gesture for Gwyn to go, the last of us before any of the girls can comment on what they've seen. I'm sure we'll talk about it, but right now I really want to get this done. I'm also curious to see what Gwyn's magic will reveal.

Her dark purple/black magic seems to shimmer as it moves forward, almost looking like a galaxy. I'm mesmerized by the sight, but I force myself to focus as it makes contact with the potion. A book comes into focus and I instantly know her power is knowledge. It clicks. She's always been so organized and just generally seems to *know* things. It then shifts into an eye, and I realize she has the power of premonition.

When it's over, we sit there in silence for a solid minute. Most of the powers that were revealed are not a surprise, but there are a few that definitely are. Speaking of which...

"Your magic is sexual?" Gwyn asks, turning to Allegra. She doesn't appear to carry the same disdain toward her as Morgan and Hazel. Maybe because she's a lesbian.

Allegra turns to her and I can see her defenses already going up. "It would seem so."

I take a look at Morgan and Hazel. Their faces look almost stricken.

"We didn't know," Morgan says, her words apologetic.

"So instead, you just thought that I'm a home-wrecking slut even though I've never been unfaithful to anyone? It's never been my fault that I get a lot of sexual attention. I've never *wanted* it. But that never mattered to you before, did it?" Her words are sharp enough to cut, and Hazel flinches as she's struck by them.

"It wasn't fair of us," Hazel says, finally seeming to find the words. "We just didn't know you properly. We thought that was the type of person you were. That you liked the attention you received. It's no excuse, but it turned us off and that's why we never took the time to get to know you."

"And we're sorry that because of that belief it affected our relationship. I realize now that it not only set the tone for how we interact, but also for how you and Gwyn interacted. She's never disliked you, but because we had our opinions about you, she never had the opportunity to get to know you," Morgan says.

These girls fucked up. But they know it, and they're admitting to it. That's something. I suddenly have a ton of admiration for Allegra. She was treated so poorly by these women, and yet, she came here. She joined our coven.

Allegra's stare is hard for long moments, but finally, her face loses that granite edge. It softens, just slightly.

"I forgive you." They are the only words she speaks, but the weight of them falls over all of us like a blanket.

I let out a breath I didn't realize I was holding. I have to admit, I was a little apprehensive about this trip. Only because I've known that there was tension between these ladies, and I didn't want there to be any unnecessary drama. Or any drama at all, really.

"So, what do you say? Can we start over?" Hazel asks hopefully.

Allegra's face softens even more. "I'd like that."

Zara squeals, scaring the shit out of us. "Oh, I'm just so happy! I feel like we need to do a bonding activity or something now."

My eyebrows rise. "That's actually not a bad idea. Does anyone have any ideas?"

"What about something with our new magic? Like an activity where we have to use all of our magic together."

"I don't know how my sex magic is going to do anything significant in a group activity other than start an orgy," Allegra says, making me laugh.

Her eyes meet mine, and we have a moment of camaraderie. I know we're going to be good friends.

"Maybe we just practice with our newly enhanced magic, then?" Gwyn asks.

I take a second to use my color magic to move the priceless, antique magical bowl out of the center of our circle. I have a feeling things are going to get rowdy, so I float it into the cabin.

Binxi also takes that moment to come out and join us.

"I wonder if I could astral project someone other than myself," Morgan muses. "I've tried in the past, but never been successful. It would probably be easier on something smaller. Mind if I try on Binxi?"

Zara looks hesitant.

"It won't hurt him. He might just be disoriented for a moment being in a different area all of a sudden," Morgan clarifies.

Zara nods, reassured.

Morgan gives her a wide smile before extending her hands toward the cat. We all gasp in amazement when a moment later, his body forms in the center of the circle. His physical body is still right where he started, but his spectral form is manifested in another area. When I look closely, I can see that he doesn't appear fully solid, but it's difficult to tell unless you know what you're looking for.

"That's amazing!" Nora cries. "What should I try to do?"

"Maybe hold your hands out and see if you can find a special stone nearby?" Gwyn suggests, a knowing glint in her eyes. She's already practicing hers, her innate wisdom and premonition giving us the guidance we need.

Nora nods excitedly, and while she does that, I go grab some herbs that I know Zara brought with us. I want to test something, and Gwyn's idea gave me my own.

I bring out what I've found, the girls all giving me curious looks. I'm also pleased to see that Nora found a quartz crystal. It has dirt on it, so she must've had to dig for it.

I sit in front of my sister, the herbs I have behind my back. "Your turn, Zar. Close your eyes and don't breathe through your nose. I want you to try and identify what these herbs are just from the energy they give off."

She nods, and I hold the purple bundle in front of her first, bringing it close without touching her. Immediately her shoulders relax and a serene expression crosses her face.

"Lavender."

"Yes!" I exclaim. I knew she'd be able to do it.

The next one I hold in front of her is a green bundle. Her brows furrow for a moment, but then it dawns on her.

"Basil. Also, we need to make sure Morgan always has that with her. It aids in astral projection."

I smile, holding up the final one. This one wasn't intended for our use, but Binxi's. I hold it so it's almost touching her hands in her lap. This one has her confused, but in the next moment Binxi jumps into her lap, stealing it from my hand.

Zara laughs loudly before exclaiming, "Catnip!"

"Me next!" Hazel exclaims.

She guides her hands to the ground underneath her and Nora gasps in amazement as a sprout begins to grow from the center of the circle.

"Are you growing something specific?" I ask.

She nods. "I'm trying to form a shape."

"Ooh, let's try and guess what it is!" Nora adds, excited by the prospect of making it a game.

"Plant!" Zara yells.

We all burst out laughing. Hazel shakes her head, a smile on her lips as she continues to grow the plant in front of us. It begins to take shape and we all start yelling out random things.

"A blob!"

"A bean!"

"A fetus!"

Hazel is fully laughing now, along with most of us, but she keeps growing it. It basically looks like a circle with a stem coming out of it, but not out of the center, it's off to the side. I'm shocked when she continues to grow it laterally. What the fuck could this thing be?

"A square!" Morgan yells. I could see that. It looks like the first half that shape, except for the weird circle thing at the bottom.

Hazel shakes her head but keeps going. She brings the vine down on the opposite side now, and none of us have any guesses, until she grows another little circle at the bottom.

"Oh! It's eighth notes!" I yell, finally seeing it.

"Music!" Gwyn shouts next to me.

"Yes!" Hazel screeches. The use of so much magic clearly exhausted her, but she looks exhilarated at the same time.

Allegra is next. She gives us all a thoughtful look before a devious smile lights her face. She stands and moves to the center of the circle.

"Let's dance," she tells us all.

Morgan and Hazel immediately jump up, looking excited at the prospect, but the rest of us are hesitant.

"I'm not a big dancer," Nora admits.

"*Dance with me*," Allegra says again, and this time, liquid sex coats her voice, making me want to follow her every command just to please her.

We all stand and move forward toward her as she starts a seductive sway. She reaches out, touching us all, and soon we're all moving together. It's heady and pure sinful. Gwyn and I move closer together, grinding against each other more than anyone else, and I can't help the lust that builds inside of me to a near unbearable level. Just as we're about to kiss, Allegra cuts off her magic. We all stop as if we've been suddenly doused with cold water.

Allegra makes her way back to her seat as if nothing happened, although she does have a smug smile on her face.

"Not quite an orgy, but the next best thing," she comments wryly.

We all chuckle although it's a little forced. Everyone shakes themselves out of her spell. It's almost painful trying to claw my way out of the lust-filled cloud, but we eventually all manage it.

I go last. Everyone told Gwyn to go, but she informed us that she's been practicing the whole time just like I knew she was. Her power is just much more subtle, but she's had that knowing look in her eyes this whole time.

I could make a potion, but I'm already so comfortable with that. What I haven't had as much experience with is blood magic. I wish I had my special bowl with me, but I left it at home, not knowing I would need it.

I try to decide what I want to do, mentally flipping through my spell book. There is one that I've always wanted to try. Conjuring. It would definitely be a useful tool to have in my arsenal.

I slit my finger open, pouring the dots of blood in a small circle. I chant low and steady, calling for the object I want to come to me. At first nothing happens, but as I continue to speak, a bottle of wine manifests in front of me.

The girls whoop in excitement and I pump my fist in the air in success.

"Well, ladies, I think we can definitely say this was a win," I say.

After our experiment, we head inside to our separate rooms, although Allegra winks and looks knowingly at Gwyn, making me blush. With her sex magic, she knows that we're interested in each other. I try not to worry about it. It's late, and we're exhausted. Zara and I collapse into bed, and while she passes out immediately, I stay awake listening to her deep breathing.

Even though I'm thoroughly spent from the events of the day, I'm exhilarated from the surge in my magic.

There's also a certain emo witch whose kisses I can't get out of my head. She and I haven't seen much of each other lately, but having her in the same house, sleeping not far away, makes me unable to think about anything else.

After lying awake for an hour, I finally give in to the pull to go to her. I sneak out of bed, even though Zara isn't a light sleeper. My bare feet are silent as I creep down the hall to her room.

I open the door with a creak. Maybe I should be knocking, but I want to see if she's even awake. When I peek my head in, she's lying on her back but propped up on her elbows.

She raises an expectant brow at me. "Are you coming in?"

My heart beats excitedly, but I stay there watching her for a moment.

"I've been waiting for you," she admits, biting her lip.

And that makes my mind up for me. I enter the room and ease the door shut behind me. All is quiet in the house, and I know we're the only two up right now. She scoots over in the small bed to make room for me.

"Are you sure about this?" I ask her. Even though minutes ago I was ready to throw caution to the wind.

She nods, wetting her lips. "I can't stop thinking about you. About your mouth on mine." She grabs my nightgown and pulls me down to her.

Before I can reply, she presses her lips to mine and I'm a goner. She tastes minty, like her toothpaste, and I moan into her mouth before covering her body with my own. She's in a skimpy tank and booty shorts, and my hands greedily skate over every inch of her. She has the smoothest skin.

I'm not wearing many clothes either, and our pebbled nipples rub against each other with every brush of our bodies. Although, hers feel harder than mine. Fire erupts in my blood, and in my excitement, I bite her lip.

She cries out in pleasure and wraps her legs around my waist, grinding against me. She breaks our kiss. "Please, Luna. I want you so bad," she begs, making wetness instantly rush to my core.

"What do you want?"

"I want to taste you. I want you to come all over my tongue."

I let out a whimper at her words and nod.

She wastes no time. She sits up, forcing me back before continuing and pushing me all the way onto my spine. In the dim light she surveys my body with greedy eyes.

"I need your clothes off. Now." She begins pulling at my nightie, and between the two of us, we have it off quickly.

"Your turn," I tell her. She smirks at me, but obliges.

My mouth waters when I see the piercings glinting on her nipples. Fuck, those are hot. Now I know why they felt so hard. Before I can stop myself, I sit up and take one into my mouth. I suck hard, earning a sharp inhale from her. A minute later, I switch to her other one, not wanting it to feel left out.

"Luna," she whines.

I smirk against her skin, but pull away. She attacks my mouth in a savage kiss, and I know I've got her all sorts of worked up. Just how I want her.

She shoves me down again, and then, her glorious mouth is on me. She leaves a wet trail from my neck all the way to my breasts, and then down my stomach before she finally reaches where I want her most.

The moment her pierced tongue makes contact with my clit, I'm a fucking goner. I run my fingers through her black locks and clutch her to me for dear life. Her chuckle vibrates against me, sending even more pleasure sparking through my body. I wrap my legs around her head, wanting her as close as I can possibly get her.

She moans as she tastes me, and I can't help but cry out at the sensations she's evoking in me. She's so good at this. Literally the best I've ever had. She switches between long, slow licks, fast flicks, and plunging her tongue inside of me. Her cool piercing feels like heaven along my heated skin, and I grind against her face, chasing my pleasure.

Within minutes, she has me detonating. I bring my nightie up to my mouth to muffle my cry of pleasure before I wake up the entire house.

When my body stops shaking and I go limp beneath her, Gwyn finally pulls back. I can see my slick glistening against her mouth and chin, and the sight makes pleasure reignite through my body. She has a satisfied smirk on her face as she leans down to give me a tender kiss. My essence permeates between us, and I'm fully aware that she's probably uncomfortable from being so worked up with no relief.

I'm about to flip her and return the favor when I feel the slickness of her cunt glide against mine. I gasp into her mouth, wanting more of her, *needing* more of her. As if she can read my mind, she breaks the kiss and straddles me sideways, our legs intertwined, and presses herself more firmly against me.

"Fuck, you're so wet," I tell her. Her arousal is leaking all over me, and I couldn't love it more if I tried.

She grips one of my legs and pulls it wider, giving her more access. All of her is pressed against all of me and I moan in renewed pleasure. I'm so sensitive from my orgasm, and it's almost too much.

Then she starts moving and I'm lost. I trail my hands up to her breasts, tweaking and playing with her nipples and tugging on her piercings. She bites her lip to keep her moan in, but it doesn't work.

The bed rocks with every movement of our hips, but I can't bring myself to care. Fuck it, let the whole house know at this point.

"I'm close again," I murmur.

"Come for me," she orders, and I'm a slave to her command.

When I come down, I notice she hasn't found release yet. I give her a questioning look.

"I want your tongue and fingers."

My mouth waters at the prospect of tasting her, and I'm quick to get up. She laughs huskily at my enthusiasm, but lies back for me.

I immediately latch on to her clit with my lips, not wanting to waste time on buildup. We've had enough of that already, and I'm eager to feel her climax for me.

She cries out as I push two fingers into her dripping cunt. I pump them hard in and out before curling my fingers to find her G-spot. She gasps, and encouraged, I do it again while flicking my tongue rapidly over her. Moments later, she's coming, clamping hard around my fingers. I moan into her pussy, the sound of her coming making me so hot.

When she's finished, I pull back, licking her off my fingers. Her eyes latch on to the action and flare with heat. I crawl up the bed and lie down next to her. She gathers me into her arms, and we drift off like that.

No one mentions our sexcapades, but it's clear they're all very aware of what's going on between us. Luckily, no one seems bothered by it. Zara does privately ask me if I want her to switch rooms with Gwyn so we can share the large bed. I take her up on it, after changing the sheets, of course.

We spend days at the cabin. We all practice our magic at every opportunity, and we are all indeed stronger. Nora is still very new, but we teach her all we can. She's a natural, and it's fun watching her grow into what she never knew she was capable of.

It's also been really refreshing to see how Allegra is interacting with the girls, especially Morgan and Hazel. It was awkward at first, but they're starting to move past it. I know they probably won't end up being best friends, but I'm relieved that they'll at least be able to get along.

Gwyn bursts into the kitchen on our last morning. "Ladies! I just had a vision while I slept."

"I think that's just called a dream, Gwyn," Allegra teases.

She ignores the comment completely. "I don't know exactly what will happen, but I know what we need to do."

"You're being incredibly vague," I tell her. "I'm going to need more detail."

She rolls her eyes at me and huffs. "Just come on. I'll explain what we need to do once we get outside." She grabs my hand and tugs me along behind her. I love the casual touch, even as sparks seem to fly up my arms, giving me goosebumps.

The rest of the girls watch us with knowing fascination, and I can feel a blush rising to my cheeks. I don't necessarily care that they know there's something going on between the two of us, but parading it in front of them is another thing entirely. I don't *dislike* it, but it is strange and new for me.

I push thoughts of that from my head as soon as we get outside, to the spot where we've been bonding and practicing our magic together. The other girls close in behind us, and we form the same circle standing in the same order that felt natural that first time.

"So, what's this about?" Hazel asks, curiosity coloring her tone.

Gwyn doesn't answer her question directly, but she instructs us all to hold our hands out to our neighbor, our palms touching, although not holding, and there's a continuous connection throughout the circle.

"Okay, now everyone release their color magic."

We do as she says, slowly at first. Morgan cries out in shock when a shimmering dome begins to form around us. It's made up of every color in our coven, almost like a rainbow, except all the colors seem to blend together whilst still remaining in their original state. It's the most bizarre thing I've ever seen, but I can also feel the potent magic coating the air surrounding us.

"What the hell is this?" I ask, my voice a whisper. As if I speak any louder it will break the spell.

"I have no idea. But it's something important. Something incredibly powerful. I sensed that in my vision."

We break the connection, and cold immediately floods my system. The lack of presence of my coven sisters' magic almost feeling like a missing limb.

"We need to figure out what this does, but I think we need outside help."

"How about Arthur and Joey?" Allegra asks.

"That would be perfect," Zara adds. "They already know we have magic and are close to us. Plus, even though they can't officially be a part of the coven since they don't have powers, I like the idea of them being involved in some way."

Allegra nods. "I'll call Arthur and let him know that they should be ready when we get back." She heads off to do just that when Morgan's phone rings.

She answers and her face pales. When she hangs up, she looks like she's seen a ghost.

"What is it, Morgan?" Hazel asks.

"My friend is missing. She's a witch too."

NINE

Zara

When we finally get back to the shop, everything feels...out of sorts. After learning that one of the local witches has gone missing, I think we're all on edge. I take a sip from my water bottle, trying to stay hydrated to calm my anxiety. Glancing at the clock, I remind myself there's only thirty minutes left 'til closing. And thank Mother, at least I don't have to close the shop alone tonight. Vik is here.

He and I have been really hitting it off lately, and it feels so good to have a man in the shop with me since witches aren't safe at the moment.

Vik walks over to me. "Zara, are you doing okay?"

I hesitate before giving a quick nod.

"That's not convincing," he says.

"I'm sorry. I'm just feeling a little freaked over one of Morgan's friends going missing."

"I'm sure it's just a coincidence that she went missing and is a witch. Maybe she's run off with a lover or something," he suggests.

I know he's only trying to comfort me, but sometimes men just don't get it. Especially men who haven't been around witches very long.

"I'd love to believe that, trust me, but it's hard to think positively when these things usually aren't a coincidence in the witchy world."

Vik nods and tosses his hands in the air. "You're right. I'm sorry I don't have the answer. I simply wish there was a way I could help put your mind at ease, love." He inches closer to me and puts his arm around my waist, pulling me into him. He gives me a big hug, and my shoulders relax. He smells so fucking good, it distracts me from worry for a second.

I breathe him in one more time before releasing the hug and looking up at him. "I just wish I wasn't so scared of being alone right now."

"Did you drive to the shop today?" he asks.

"Yeah, why?"

"Just curious. I'm glad you won't be walking home alone tonight." He turns his head and looks out the window at the pitch-black parking lot.

"You can say that again," I say.

"How about you leave your car here tonight, and I'll drive you home? Just to

make sure you're not alone."

I contemplate his suggestion for a moment, thinking how nice it would be to have company when I get back to the house and how I can't help but want to be alone at my place with Vik. Luna is staying with Gwyn, so we won't have to tiptoe around her.

"Yes, please. I'd appreciate that," I tell him.

"Good. Then it's settled."

I smile before making my way over to the door to shut down for the night. I see someone standing outside, so I open it slightly.

My eyes meet those familiar, sharp green eyes. It's the woman who was staring at me through the shop window the last time Vik and I worked together.

Feeling spooked, I quickly close the door, lock it, and switch the Open sign to Closed. When I turn around, Vik eyes me suspiciously.

"You all right?" he asks.

I let out a deep breath. "Did you see that woman outside?"

He shakes his head. "No, I'm sorry, I didn't. Who was it?"

"I have no clue, but she freaks me out. It's been twice that I've caught her staring at me now. I definitely don't want her in the shop. For all I know, she's the one who took Morgan's friend."

"Hey," he says, moving closer to me, grabbing my upper arms and rubbing them gently. It instantly soothes me. "You're okay. I'm here. Is there anything else I can do to help calm your nerves?"

"You know what? I just remembered that Nora gifted all us girls a crystal at the retreat, and mine is supposed to help bring calm energy. I'm gonna go grab it from the Moon Room real quick."

"The what room?" Vik asks me.

My lips part open. "You've worked here for how long now and don't know about the Moon Room?" I ask.

He shakes his head. "Am I supposed to know?" Amusement and something else I can't identify coloring his features.

I take a moment to process if he'd ever need to go down there with us. "I guess it is more so strictly coven-related stuff, so that does make sense you've not needed to be down there. It's super cool though."

"Oh, nice," he replies. "Can I see it?"

"Hmm, ya know, I don't see why not. I mean, you work here and know us already, so it's not like it's a secret." I continue to debate out loud, "I really don't think it'd hurt anything. Let's go check it out."

"If you insist," he says as usual. I can't help but smile.

I head over to the shelves and rub the silver crescent moon. The shelf swings open and I step onto the staircase to head downstairs.

"Well, that's incredible," Vik remarks.

"Right?" I say. "Come on."

Vik's foot thrusts forward but stops midair.

"What are you doing?" I ask.

He repeats the motion with the other foot. "That's weird. I can't step on the staircase."

"Wait, really?" I ask. "Try one more time."

He firmly plants both feet on the ground and releases a breath before trying to take another step. No luck.

"What the hell?" I say. "It doesn't make any sense."

"Maybe only coven members are allowed in?" he asks me.

I nod, pondering it for a moment. "But Joey has come in before..."

His eyes harden. "Oh?"

"Yeah. Weird." I take a moment to decide if I should get the damn crystal later. "You know, let's not stress it. I'll be super quick. Be right back," I say before turning to hurry down the stairs and grab the crystal from my seat at the coven table. It takes me only a few seconds, and when I see the coven journal, it hits me that you'd have to be a descendant to enter the room. Which is why Joey can come down here, but not Vik. I blow out a breath and make it back to the shop.

Vik is still at the top waiting for me. "Did you get what you needed?" he asks.

"Sure did. And it occurred to me that Joey is a descendant of the original coven, so maybe you have to be related by blood to enter." I don't know for sure if this is even true, but it makes me feel better since I don't want Vik to be jealous of Joey.

I rub the crystal and do a brief inhale-exhale exercise to try to stay calm.

"That makes sense," he says, watching me as I close the hidden passageway.

"I'm sorry. I hope you're not upset with me. I didn't mean to hype it up just for you to not even be able to go down there."

He waves a hand. "It's not your fault at all. And it's all right. I'm still worried about you though. Let's get you home."

I nod and look at the hidden entryway a final time, ensuring it's completely shut. "Yeah, you're right. Let's get out of here."

After a brief tour of the house, I look at him. "So, that's pretty much it."

"It's very nice," he says and gives me that sexy grin of his.

"Thanks. At first I was worried it was going to feel too big for us, or that it might be awkward not having my grandma here, but it's working out nicely. Especially since neither of us have to sleep in her room or anything."

His gold-speckled green eyes stare into mine. "Well, I personally think it's great that you've kept her room in place. I never met her, but I think she'd appreciate it. I know I sure would."

"That's how Luna and I felt too. Felt respectful," I say.

Vik clears his throat. "Speaking of respectful, young lady... I better let you get some rest. Thanks for letting me take you home to make sure you got here safe and sound."

I let out a brief chuckle. "Ah, my protector."

He begins to make his way toward the front door. "I'll see you at work," he says.

I know I really need rest right now, but something pulls me to ask, "Wait. I'm probably going to have a glass of wine before bed. Want to join me?"

He pauses and his eyes squint. "Are you sure?"

"I insist," I say teasingly.

"All right, then, if you insist," he says before giving me a wink.

My heart rate speeds up a bit at the thought of what this night might turn into for us. I haven't had sex since Chad, and I'm dying to know what it's like to have Viktor inside of me. Just looking at him gets me wet, so I can only imagine how amazing it'd be to go all the way with him. I feel like he'd probably teach me a thing or two.

"Great," I say. "Please make yourself at home, and I'll go grab us the wine. Is red okay with you?"

"More than okay," he responds. Vik plops down on the couch and I scurry over to the kitchen to grab us a bottle.

I select one of my favorites before grabbing two wine glasses and returning to the living room.

I pour us each a glass and take my seat on the couch next to him. We've hung out several times before, and there's always been chemistry, but for some reason, I start to worry that maybe he isn't into me at all. Will this end awkwardly? I mean, he did agree to have a glass of wine with me. He could've said no.

I set my wineglass down on the coffee table and tuck a strand of hair behind my ear. His eyes catch mine as he sets his glass down as well.

"The wine is delicious," he says. My eyes flick to his mouth at the word *delicious*. He notices and bites his bottom lip.

Before my mind starts to wander further down a rabbit hole of worries, he leans in and kisses me. My lips part and his tongue meets mine. His hand makes its way to my hair and he tugs it softly before slowly moving it to my neck. He takes my lower lip between his teeth and I release a whimper.

"But not as delicious as you," he murmurs as he pulls back for a moment.

I lie back on the couch, pulling him on top of me and his lips back to mine. My fingers explore their way through his sexy dark hair as he continues to thrust his tongue in and out of my mouth, occasionally biting my lower lip. After a few moments, he shifts and I take a deep breath.

"Want to go to my room?" I ask.

"Thought you'd never ask," he says. I try to act super seductive and grab ahold of his hand, leading him into my room.

When we arrive, Binxi is lying on the top of my bed. I try to coax him off of it, and he stubbornly takes his sweet time making his way to the floor. After not one, but two stretches, he lands on the ground with a thud before slowly walking over to the corner and facing us directly.

Vik laughs. "I think he's gonna watch us."

"Probably," I say and start to chuckle.

"Well, forget him. Where were we?" he asks before pulling me down with him on top of the bed. He presses his lips against mine and I push my breasts up against his chest and roll on top of him. He releases my lips and looks at me before softly dragging his finger over my chest, teasing me. After a moment, I tug at his shirt and pull it up over his arms and shoulders. Once completely off, I toss it to the floor and stare at his drop-dead gorgeous abs. Not to mention the tattoos that seem to be covering every inch of him. "Seriously?" I say, and he laughs.

"I take care of my body. Just like I'm about to take care of yours," he says, taking my shirt off. Before I even realize it, my bra is off as well and my nipple in his mouth. He suckles and I release a moan. My body squirms in hunger for him as he makes his way to my other breast. He releases it with a pop before looking at both and smiling devilishly at their hardness.

I exhale slowly and watch as his eyes narrow. "Fuck me, Vik," I say.

"With pleasure, miss," he says. He stares at me with an intensity I've never experienced before. He slides me gently over to his side and begins to undo the belt buckle of his jeans. I remain focused on his bulge, excited for what's to come, when he leans over me and starts messing around near my nightstand. "What are you doing?" I ask.

"Just looking for a condom," he says.

"Oh, I'm on birth control, so we're all good there. Are you clean? 'Cause I am," I say before attempting to draw him back into a kiss.

He pulls back and still fumbles around in the nightstand.

"Did you hear me?" I ask, thinking maybe he's so focused on finding a condom, he tuned me out.

He doesn't respond, so I sit up to see what the hell is happening. He's messed up the entire organization of my drawer, but before I can say something, Binxi is back on the bed with us.

"Binxi's ba—" I start to say, but I'm interrupted by a shout from Viktor. My eyes widen as Binxi leaps onto Viktor's chest, digging his claws right into him. I try to pull Binxi off, but he climbs up more and bites Vik right on the nipple.

I cry out in shock. "Damn, Binxi, you've never acted like this before." I attempt to pull him off, but Viktor pushes him down to the floor. I let out a whimper, but Binxi scurries off the next moment though, and I know he's fine. I look back to find Vik's chest laden with cat scratches and nipple gushing with blood.

"What the hell?" he says before cursing more under his breath.

"You okay?" I grab some tissues and shake my head. "I have seriously never seen him act like that before."

"I'm fine."

"You sure?" I ask, realizing Binxi may have interfered with the potentially best sex of my life. "How can I help?"

"You've done enough," he snaps. He releases a loud exhale and looks at me. "I'm sorry, I didn't mean that. I just need a minute."

"Oh yeah, for sure," I say. My hand covers my mouth as bile rises in my throat. I run to the bathroom to vomit, but nothing comes out. When I head back into the bedroom, I see no sign of Viktor. His V-neck is no longer on the floor.

"Vik?" I call out. No response.

As I make my way down the hall, I finally see him. His hand on the doorhandle of Granny Lizzie's bedroom.

"What are you doing?' I ask and grip the wall, trying to stabilize myself. Hopefully I don't projectile vomit on him right now.

"Oh, um, yeah. I was just looking for another bathroom since you were in yours," he says.

"Shit, I'm sorry about that. I felt a bit nauseous for a moment, but I think I'm good now. I still can't wrap my head around Binxi acting like that. He usually loves people."

"Yeah, it's fine," he says, the words not matching up with the darkness in his eyes. "I'm going to go. I need to get some air."

I want to console him and ask him to stay, but the room begins to spin as I stand there, watching him leave.

Maybe I just need sleep. This whole situation has thrown me off, and I don't feel so hot. I head back to my room and lie down before closing my eyes. I focus on my breathing when my eyes open to the sound of a knock at our door.

I rise to my feet, trying to stay grounded and ignore the dizzy spell. I pause at the front door. I hope Vik can forgive me and Binxi.

"I was hoping you'd come back," I say as I open the door. But to my surprise, it's not Vik. "Joey? What are you doing here?" I ask. I normally feel so relieved to see him, but in the moment, I'm annoyed. I need to talk to Vik, not him.

He runs his fingers through his gelled brown hair. "I, uh, well, I came to talk. Got a minute?"

"I guess so. What's up?"

He sighs. "Do you mind if I come in?"

"Sure." I hold the door open for him. "Make yourself at home," I say, trying to feel like myself again.

"Thanks," he says, taking a seat on the couch. "I hope I'm not wrong to tell you this, but I felt like it might be weird if you heard it from someone else. But, I broke up with Tiffany."

My heart does a tiny leap in my chest. "Oh?" I sit down on the couch next to him, and remind myself, *Girl, you were just about to have sex with Vik. And he is so damn sexy. It's too late to try to start anything with Joey.*

"Yeah, we just have grown apart and she's a lot different than she used to be." He clears his throat. "Don't get me wrong, I am too. I think we all change so much, and sometimes our partners change in different ways than we do, and it makes people less compatible."

I nod. "Yeah, I understand. I think anyway. I've never really had a long enough relationship to know."

"Well, that's another reason I'm here." He shifts his body a bit before inching closer to me on the couch. "I have feelings for you, Zar. I have for a while now, but out of respect for my relationship with Tiffany, I never acted on them."

"What? For real?" I ask. "But we're just friends now, right?"

His eyebrows rise and he scratches the back of his head. "Um, yeah. Totally. I just—I thought there might be something more between us."

"Oh yeah. I'm sorry you thought that. I'm actually with Vik now."

He laughs. "That creepy dude? You're joking, right?"

"Excuse me?" I say, feeling defensive. He was with self-centered Tiffany for so long and has the nerve to judge me. "No, I'm not joking. And we're getting a bit serious now too."

"Zar," he says and takes a deep breath. "I'm not judging you. You, of course, can date whoever you want, and I want you to be happy. But that guy gives me the creeps for some reason."

My left eyebrow rises in suspicion. "How?"

"Well, for one thing, when you all were at the coven retreat, I dropped by the shop a few times to check on things, and he was acting really strange."

My arms fold across my chest. "Strange, how? Still waiting on you to tell me what makes him seem so creepy."

"I can't explain it, really. I just get bad vibes from him. It seemed like he was being too nosy in the shop for someone who works there. Like snooping around and shit, ya know?"

I laugh. "Sounds like someone is maybe a bit jealous?"

He tosses his hands in the air as though he's about to get arrested. "Zar, I like you a lot, I do. But I'm not the jealous type. I really just want to make sure you're happy...and safe."

"I appreciate it, but I've made up my mind. I did like you too, but I'm with Vik now, and that's who I'm choosing. Thanks for coming by," I say, standing to my feet.

He stands and looks at me, his brown eyes soft. I do believe he cares about me, but I can't do this to Vik right now. We were just about to have sex, for Mother's sake.

"For what it's worth, I am sorry I missed my chance with you, but I really do wish you and Vik all the best. You deserve to be happy and have everything your heart wants, Zar."

"Thanks," I say before walking him over to the door. "Well, thanks for stopping by. I'll see ya around."

Joey forces a half smile before giving me a stiff, awkward wave. I want to joke with him that the awkward wave is usually my thing, but his back is already to me as he heads back to his truck in the driveway.

I shut the door and lean against it, feeling relieved that he's gone so I can finally settle my stomach and get some rest. Alone.

TeN

Luna

It's one of those rare days when neither I nor Zara have to work, and I have to admit, it's refreshing. The only time both of us get the day off together is when either Gwyn or Viktor are working. That being said, Zara and I both like to be at the shop often to ensure that everything is running smoothly. And if I'm being completely honest, I don't trust Viktor. I know Zara does, so I'm *trying* to give him the benefit of the doubt, but her track record isn't the best. I mean look at Chad. I mean, Binxi.

"So, how are things going between you and Vik?" I ask.

"Well, I brought him home the other night..."

My eyebrows fly up in surprise. It's not like my sister is a prude or anything, quite the opposite, I think, remembering her lingerie incident with Chad, but she's a romantic and sometimes likes to take her time.

"Where was I?"

"At Gwyn's," she says, and I detect just a flicker of snippiness from her.

That's weird and completely out of character for her. Me? Absolutely. Her? Absolutely not. I brush it off. Maybe she's had a bad day or something, and Crone knows I've snapped at her for no reason whatsoever. She basically owes me at this point.

"Oh, okay. So, what happened?"

"Well, we started fooling around, and before we could actually *do the thing*, Binxi freaked out and attacked him. He pounced on him and started scratching the shit out of his chest. He even bit his nipple."

Zara is so serious, but the image that appears in my head is priceless. I burst out laughing, wine coming out of my nose.

"Luna! It's not funny! Viktor was really upset!"

Zara's face makes me laugh even harder, and I struggle to get myself back under control. Three-Faced Goddess. If I didn't know I was an evil bitch before, I do now. Laughing at other people's pain is just wrong, but I can't help myself. Tears are streaming down my face, but Zara just glares at me.

Finally, I pull myself back together. "I'm sorry. That image just kept replaying in my head and I couldn't stop."

Zara huffs and rolls her eyes, which sobers me instantly. It's so unlike my sister that it immediately puts me on edge.

"*Anyway*, he was very upset, and now I don't know what to do. Why doesn't Binxi like him?"

I shift uncomfortably. Now might be the time to tell her, but I don't think it will go over very well.

Her eyes latch on to the movement and she's immediately suspicious. "What is it?"

"What do you mean?" I ask, deflecting.

"You never fidget. What did you do?"

I sigh. "Okay. See, the thing is, I didn't exactly find Binxi."

"Stop being cryptic! What did you do?" she yells, and I'm stunned. I don't know if she's *ever* yelled at me before.

"I turned Chad into Binxi. I think that's why he is attacking Viktor. I'm pretty sure he's jealous. Not that he remembers he's Chad anymore, but it could just be an instinctual thing."

She stares at me in disbelief. I blush under her scrutiny.

"Wait a minute. You *what*?!"

I resist the urge to curl in on myself. I had my reasons for doing what I did, and I stand by them. "Hey! That asshole deserved it!"

"We took care of it!"

"Giving him a mild STD that he could clear up with antibiotics does not count as taking care of it. He wouldn't have learned his lesson and would've done the same thing to more girls in the future." Not that I actually care about the other girls, but I know Zara, and her bleeding heart would go out to those other women.

"How *dare* you. You had *no right* to do that! And then to bring him in here and let me fall in love with him!"

"Well, he doesn't remember anything! He didn't retain any of his human memories or attributes."

"That doesn't make it okay, Luna! You've overstepped. How did you even change him?"

Fuck. She's not going to like this answer. I'm not ashamed of the type of magic I do, but I know this is going to strike a nerve with her.

"I used blood magic."

"You mean to tell me that you used what our old coven labeled as 'dark magic'? That's why we got kicked out in the first place, wasn't it? I thought all this time that it was because we hexed him, but that wasn't it at all, was it? You broke the coven's laws, and because of it, you uprooted our entire lives!"

My anger spikes. "You didn't even want to be there anymore. The coven had nothing to do with us moving here and you know it."

She doesn't even address what I said, instead, she revisits our previous topic of discussion. "You need to change him back."

My eyes widen. She loves that cat. She's not thinking clearly. I know that if she was, she wouldn't be willing to give him up so easily. She's thinking of him as Chad and not as Binxi. The fact is that they're no longer the same. Chad changed as soon as I spelled him.

"No," I tell her. I won't change him back.

She stares at me with accusation and distrust. "Then I have nothing else to say to you." She walks away without another word, crushing my heart under her feet.

The next week is tense. Zara and I rarely see each other, and when we do, she doesn't even meet my eyes or speak to me unless absolutely necessary. We take opposite shifts at the shop, and the times that we aren't working, I try to spend at Gwyn's.

Gwyn notices after a few days. "What's going on with you and Zara?"

"What do you mean?" I ask, deflecting. I've never been great at the whole communication thing.

She levels me with a look that says she can see through my bullshit. Even though we haven't known each other long at all, she's extremely perceptive and has the power of premonition. She's come to learn my tells and personality quirks more quickly than I expected. It's not a bad thing, but it is something I'm not used to. Zara is really the only one who's had that ability in the past. And the only one who has cared. Until now. *Fuck.* My heart sinks.

"Okay, spit it out, bitch. What's bothering you?"

I heave a heavy sigh. "Zara and I had a big fight. And now she's not talking to me."

"About what?"

I tell her everything. I expect her to be disturbed by what I've done, or at least unnerved, but she doesn't even bat an eye. Mother, this woman is perfect for me. She just listens intently, giving me her full attention.

"Well, I would guess that it's a bit of a shock for her right now. She probably just needs to come to terms with everything. Give her time. She'll come around eventually."

It's sound advice, but I can't shake the feeling that something is off. Zara and I have had fights before. We're sisters who live together. *Of course*, we've had fights before. But never like this. Never where we didn't resolve it within a day or two. Never where she didn't even *look* at me.

I nod anyway, not knowing what else to say or do. At this point, I don't think there's anything I *can* do.

"You're probably right."

"Also, you guys have been so stressed and busy. You've gone through a ton of changes recently, and while they've all been good, any modifications like this are difficult."

I sigh again, but relent. "Well, what should I do for our next coven meeting? It's going to be awkward."

She chuckles. "There will be enough of us there that it will be fine. I'll be your buffer," she replies, giving me a slight hip bump.

I crowd her space, pushing her up against the counter behind her. "Oh, so you want to buff me now?"

She laughs, pushing against my chest lightly. I don't back up, instead, I capture her mouth with mine, thoroughly distracting us both.

A few days later, we have our next coven meeting. Unusual nerves bubble in my stomach at the thought of interacting with my sister. I rarely ever get nervous, but I don't want her to start anything with me in front of the others, or to potentially turn them against me. I never would think that about Zara normally, but she's *not* acting normally. In fact, I feel like I don't even recognize her.

Unfortunately, we have to sit next to each other for the meeting since that's our typical seating arrangement. The silver lining is that we at least don't have to look at each other. The other ladies notice, but luckily they don't say anything.

The meeting commences as normal, and we take care to practice our magic together, twining it with each other's. The more familiar that our magic becomes with each other, the stronger we will be, and the quicker we'll bond. We, of course, have already done this before, but it gets stronger and more resilient and solidified with every meeting.

We blow out the candles and leave the Moon Room, planning on hanging out in the lobby with some wine for a while. It's become a tradition for us, and even though things aren't good between me and Zara, this routine and camaraderie between us all is comforting. I soak it up with everything in me.

When we're on our second glass of wine, Zara takes out her phone, scrolling and texting. A smile graces her face, and I'm sure it's Vik on her screen. But when she goes back to scrolling, her face pales.

"Maiden, Mother, Crone," she whispers, horror coating her words.

"What is it?" I ask, shooting over to her. No matter what is going on between us, I will always be there for her.

She tilts her phone toward me so I can see the screen.

Woman in Salem Missing.

I read the short article, but besides the horrible fact that a woman has been kidnapped, or worse, I don't see why it's affected her so.

"She came into the shop. She's a local witch who bought some stuff from me. We chatted for a while. According to the article, that was the last day she was seen."

I can feel the blood drain from my face. "Are you sure that's her?"

If looks could kill...

"Of course I'm sure. Not only do I recognize her face and name, but I took note of the little moon birthmark she had on her eyebrow." She points to the picture, and sure enough, I see the mark she's talking about.

"This seems to be becoming a pattern," Morgan comments from across the room. "Remember another one went missing when we went on the retreat?"

All of us glance around worriedly at each other. "Do you think someone is targeting the Salem witches?" I ask.

Zara gasps, and everyone glances to her.

"What is it?" I ask.

"I just remembered that the day this witch went missing I saw an extremely strange woman outside the shop. She was staring right at me, and I saw her again the other day. I wonder if she's responsible for the disappearances."

Chills erupt over my skin. "What did she look like?"

"I didn't get the best look at her, but she had auburn hair and bright green eyes."

"Maybe we're reading too much into this. It's only been two so far. But if there are any more we'll know for sure," Gwyn pipes in.

"What do we do in the meantime?" Nora asks, anxiety lacing her tone.

"For now, everyone be extremely vigilant, and Gwyn and I will do some research to see if we can find some way to protect us all. It will be difficult because we don't know where these women are going or who's taking them, but I'll see what I can find," I reassure everyone.

They all nod nervously. We continue the evening, but the mood has been ruined. We all go our separate ways, and I'm plunged back into awkwardness when I have to drive back home with Zara. Gwyn wants to have a night to herself, and while I understand, I'm not looking forward to spending the night at home with Zara and then working our shift together tomorrow.

I wonder if I should try to talk to her about everything again, but I have a feeling that at this point it will make things worse. I keep Gwyn's advice in mind, giving her time and space to settle down.

When we get home, we both go to our rooms, and even though it's tense being in the same house as Zara, I have to admit I needed a break from everyone.

The next morning, we head in together, Zara still not speaking to me. Whatever. That's fine.

We open the shop, but it's fairly slow. I take the opportunity to restock some of our potions. Interestingly enough, they've been one of our biggest sellers.

"I'll be in the Workshop if you need me," I tell my sister. She doesn't even respond, and I resist the urge to snap at her. Instead, I just turn and roll my eyes to myself.

I get some potions going in the back, making sure we'll have enough for the next week, and while they're cooking, I flip through my spell book. I need to see if I can find anything that will either help me find the missing witches, or protect our coven. Hopefully both. I've looked through this book a million times, but there are so many spells and potions that I forget what's actually in here. I can also check the coven journal to see if there's anything helpful in there.

Hours later, the potions are complete, but I'm still searching. Until finally, *finally*, I find something. I almost pass right over it, but it tugs at me. It's a potion specifically for those with mind magic. It not only amplifies their power, but it also allows them to project what they're seeing for everyone else. I know someone with mind magic. Someone very close to me, in fact. The only problem is I don't know how we'll be able to trigger specifically what we're looking for. I read through all the instructions when that answer comes to me as well.

If you're attempting to trigger a specific vision, speak the words of what you intend to see as you combine your color magic with the potion.

My heart beats excitedly in my chest. This is what we need. I pull my cell phone out to text Gwyn.

> Need you at the shop immediately. I found something.

Three little dots appear, and I'm incredibly grateful I don't have to track her down.

> Be over in five.

While I wait for her, I line up everything that we'll need on the counter and get the base of the potion started.

Gwyn shows up just as the base starts bubbling. She's a little later than she said she would be, which makes me even happier that I started the potion before she arrived. Now that I found it, I'm extremely impatient to get things going.

"Sorry I'm late. What did you find?"

I show her the book and she reads over everything carefully. I expect her to jump up and down with joy. Or at least give me a high five, or a smile, or *something*. Instead, she looks hesitant.

"I don't know about this, Lu."

"What do you mean? What could go wrong? It'll show us the missing witches. And the potion is fairly straightforward."

"I can't explain it, but I just have a bad feeling about it."

"Oh, come on. Don't pull a Zara on me," I tease. "Everything will be fine. It's straightforward. Nothing can go wrong."

She huffs a laugh, some of the tension easing from her. "Okay. What do you need from me?"

Excitement pounds through me. This is going to work. I know it.

"I just need a few drops of your blood, and then once the potion is finished, I'll need you to mix your color magic in as you say what you want to see."

She nods, holding her finger out to me. I prick her finger and she holds it over the boiling liquid. As it connects, a hiss emits. I quickly add in the rest of the ingredients with my color magic, lining them up in a row to dump one by one into the pot.

"Do we have to wait long?" Gwyn asks softly, as if noise will disturb the process.

I shake my head. "No, luckily this is a fairly quick potion. It only needs to boil for ten minutes while being stirred continuously."

Once everything is added, we start a timer and I get my magic to begin stirring.

It feels like the longest ten minutes in the world.

Eventually the timer goes off and I breathe a sigh of relief. Everything looks as it should.

"Ready?" I ask Gwyn.

She nods, holding her hands out in front of her.

"Do it."

She releases her dark purple magic, and it swirls amid the liquid. "Show us the missing witches."

We both gasp simultaneously as her smoke floats above the cauldron and an image starts to take shape. It's hard to see at first, but it soon becomes clear. There's a basement. It looks almost clinical. Cages line the perimeter of the room, two of them occupied by women. The missing witches. They're both unconscious and look dirty, but I can see that they're breathing. My heart shatters at the sight. I wasn't anticipating *this*.

Before we can tell if there are any identifying landmarks or *anything* we can use to find them, the smoke starts to vanish.

"No. Fuck."

We didn't even gain anything from it, other than the two witches who are missing are definitely connected and being kept by someone. No way to find them.

"At least we know they're still alive," Gwyn remarks, although I can hear the tears in her voice.

I'm about to embrace her, when I hear something behind me. I turn to see the door that was very much shut a minute ago cracked open. I bolt toward it just in time to see a woman rushing out the front door of the shop. She runs down the street and I chase after her. Her red hair is flowing in the wind and she looks over her shoulder. Her green eyes lock with mine before she faces forward, putting on another burst of speed. Fuck. I don't work out and cannot keep up with her.

I stop to catch my breath before returning to the shop. Gwyn is pacing when I enter. "Did you get her?"

I shake my head.

"Do you know who she was?"

"I think it was the woman Zara described that's been watching her and the shop. She was spying on us and saw us looking for the witches before she took off. It has to be her that's responsible, right? Why else would she run like that?"

Gwyn bites her lip worriedly. "Should we contact the authorities?"

"What are we going to say? We don't even know who the woman is, where to find her, or even have any evidence that she's actually connected to the disappearances. Not to mention we can't mention using our magic to see the captives."

She looks disappointed but nods.

"If we're going to find them, we need to do it ourselves," I state resolutely. "This is coven business."

She sighs, but nods again. "Come on, let's go clean up the Workshop."

I follow her until I hear Zara cursing. With everything that happened in the last hour or so, I completely forgot she was here.

"Go check on her, I'll take care of the shop."

"Thanks. Just don't toss the potion. Save it for me. I don't know if we'll be able to reuse it, but we might."

I follow Zara's voice to the entrance to the Moon Room. What is she doing over here?

I creep around the corner, spying on her. With the state of our relationship right now, there's a chance she won't answer me if I ask her straight up.

She has the Moon Room open and is pushing her color magic at it, muttering words I can't hear under her breath. I look around the shop to see that it's thankfully empty, but it's so out of character for her to be doing this out in the open while the customers could see.

My eyes stray to the window as I wonder if that red-haired woman's presence has anything to do with her strange behavior, but she's nowhere to be seen.

I continue watching her. She gets more and more frustrated as her attempts are apparently unsuccessful. She curses loudly, which is also somewhat out of character for her. Not that she doesn't ever do it, but there's usually a good reason for it. Especially when she drops the F bomb like she just did.

I'm about to come out and ask her what's going on, but then she's moving toward the shelf. My brows furrow as she starts prying at the crescent moon with her fingernails.

"Come *off*, Goddess damn you!"

Crone, she's trying to rip the fuckin' thing off the shelf. I step forward finally. I don't think she'll be able to manage it, but I don't want her to do any damage to herself.

"Zara, what the hell are you doing?"

Her head snaps up and her eyes meet mine. For a second they almost look glazed over but in the next moment they blaze with fury and I wonder if I'm imagining things.

"None of your business, Luna."

My head snaps back in shock as if she slapped me. Zara has *never* talked to me this way before.

My temper rises to meet hers. "It *is* my business when you're messing with the shop and the Moon Room."

She huffs, rolling her eyes at me. Who the fuck is this? "Well, I don't see why I need to justify my actions to you, but for your information, Vik can't come down into the Moon Room with me. I'm trying to change the wards to allow him access."

I just stare at her for a moment, trying to process her words. "Zara, he *shouldn't* be down there. That's coven business, and he's not part of our coven."

"But Joey was able to go down there, and you didn't have an issue with him."

"Because Joey is a descendant! If he were born female, he *would've* been in the coven with us. Vik is an outsider."

Her face contorts in rage. "An *outsider*?! He's my boyfriend!"

It takes everything in me to control the snort that wants to slip free. Zara has never had the best taste in men, so the fact that she's claiming he can come in because he's her boyfriend is laughable. Somehow I refrain from saying that though. Instead, I switch topics.

"Why are you doing this, Zara? You aren't acting like yourself."

"You're just saying that because I didn't come to you for permission first and that bothers you! You want to be in charge of everything all the time. You're the oldest, so you always get the final say on every single thing that we do. Well, this is my shop too, and I want my boyfriend to be able to come down there with me!" She's yelling by this point.

I take a moment to calm myself so I don't shout back at her. That will help nothing, even though her words cut deep. All I've ever tried to do is take care of her.

"Well, good luck trying. Gran's magic is strong and we have no idea what wards she put up to restrict access to the Moon Room. You won't be able to break it."

Without another word, I walk back to the Workshop, leaving my sister behind like she so clearly wants.

Zara

"I 'm taking a break," I yell before pushing through the shop door. I walk with haste down the sidewalk, wanting to get as far away from the shop as possible right now. Anger flows through my veins.

Seriously, what the fuck is Luna's problem? She has been the biggest bitch lately, and I can't take it any longer. I'm finally going to focus on myself. And Viktor. I deserve happiness and to not let Luna constantly trying to control me. How dare she turn Chad into a cat? Yeah, he was fucking awful, but she doesn't need to constantly solve all my problems.

I stop in front of a local bar, thinking how much I could use a drink right now. I haven't been able to shake this dizzy, uneasy feeling I've had for days, and I think it's my nerves. I've been so on edge, and all these arguments with Luna are not helping.

I step through the door and make my way right up to the bar, taking a seat in the middle of an almost-empty row. There's a couple seated together at the end, and they look so sweet, gazing into each other's eyes. See? That's all I want—passion, excitement, and chemistry. And I know I have that with Viktor. And if Luna can't see that, it's not my problem. She's off with Gwyn anyway, so why the hell does she even give a shit what I'm doing?

The burly man with soft eyes greets me from behind the bar. "Hey, little lady, what can I get started for you?" he asks.

I am in no mood to make a decision. Waving my hand in front of me, I say, "You know what? Surprise me."

His eyebrows rise to his hairline. "Not even going to give me a clue of what you like and don't like?" he asks.

"She'll take a gin and tonic," a familiar deep voice behind me says. A warmth spreads throughout my body and right between my thighs at the sound.

"Coming right up," the man says before turning around to grab the bottle of gin.

"Actually, make that two," Vik calls out before looking at me. "Hope that's okay with you?"

I nod slowly, feeling elated that he's shown up at the perfect time. Vik seats himself next to me, and I nudge him with my elbow. "If you insist," I say, smiling from ear to ear.

He puts an arm around my lower back and draws me closer to him. I nuzzle under his neck for a moment as the bartender sets the two glasses of gin and tonic on the table. "Here you both are. Anything else I can grab for you?"

"No, thank you," we answer in unison.

I laugh. "I'm loving this surprise, but what are you doing here?"

He glances at his watch. "I was in the neighborhood, thought I'd stop by and see you at the shop, but you weren't there. Luna let me know you went for a walk. So, I walked until I saw you through the window here."

"Oh, well, I'm glad you're here. It's been a day," I admit and take a sip of the drink.

"I've actually been meaning to speak with you ever since the other evening. I know we've been texting a bit, but I feel like this is an in person discussion. With how upset I got over the situation, I wanted to give you some space. And I do believe an apology is warranted on my behalf. I think the ol' bite on the nip from Binxi really rattled me," he says.

If only Luna were here to hear this. This man is seriously amazing. How can she not see it? Maybe she is a bad judge of character when it comes to guys because she's into women. Who knows? All I do know is that he makes me so happy. And horny. Oof, this dude could take shots of this gin and tonic off my body if he asked right now.

"Do you forgive me?" he asks, jolting me from my thoughts.

"Of course I do."

We lock eyes and my insides melt.

"Oh, I'm so relieved," he says. "I truly couldn't help but think of what an idiot I'd made of myself."

"You're definitely not an idiot," I say before I start to hiccup. Using my hand to cup my mouth, I suddenly can't stop the hiccups from coming.

Vik lets out a chuckle. "I don't mean to laugh, but are you all right?"

I nod, when I start to feel a bit dizzy again. Looking to my near-empty glass, I say, "Shit. I think this drink is already hitting me."

"Bit of a lightweight, hm?"

I nod and we both laugh. He puts his arm around me again, and I realize that we *are* a cute couple. He makes me feel so damn good.

The bartender turns around and looks at our drinks. "You guys ready for round two?"

I look to Vik for encouragement. He raises his hands in the air. "Up to you, but aren't you supposed to be working?"

"Shit," I say. "Yeah, I completely blanked for a second that I'm actually still on the clock. I better get going."

"Want me to walk you back?" he asks.

Before I can think about it, I answer yes. He motions for the check.

"I'm going to use the restroom quickly," I tell him before making my way to the one stall located in the back. I need to snap out of this. Whatever *this* is. After splashing myself with cold water and drying off with the roughest paper towels ever made, I open the door. Someone else is waiting, and I do a double take. I'm pretty sure it's the creepy woman who I keep seeing everywhere. Although, not everywhere, really. Mostly whenever I'm at the shop. Is she watching me? Following me?

I go to walk around her, but she bolts into the bathroom. The familiar chill shoots down my spine, and I do a little body shake.

Vik must've noticed because when I reach his side, he asks me, "You all right?"

"Yeah, I just haven't been feeling like myself lately, but I'm fine. It's shit with Luna. Sister stuff, really. No big deal."

"Don't worry, little miss, I'm here," he says before wrapping his arms around me. "Would you like to have dinner at my house tonight after work?"

I swoon and nod. "Nothing would make me happier."

It's got to be in here somewhere, I tell myself as I open up the drawers in a table in the Moon Room. "Where is it?" I whisper to myself as I pull out even more random items, like old pens and lotions and herbs that look like they've been in there for hundreds of years.

I attempt to close the drawer, but it jams. I let out a frustrated huff when I hear someone else's breath behind me. The hairs on the back of my neck rise.

"What the hell do you think you're doing?" Luna asks.

I finally get the drawer to shut and slowly turn around. I stay still as she scans my body with her eyes.

When I don't respond, she asks again, "What are you doing?" Her body shifts as she places a hand on her hip. She's pissed.

"I was just looking for—" *Wait, what was I looking for?* "I don't know," I admit.

"Really, you don't know? Like, I'm just supposed to believe that you've destroyed the entire room to find something and you don't even know what you're looking for."

I pause. "Yes. Because I don't know."

She scoffs. "Zara, enough of this shit." She looks all around the room, and I follow her gaze. It's a mess. Everything is open and the entire Moon Room is in disarray.

Luna shakes her head and lets out a sigh. "We really do need to talk, but first, please tell me what is going on with you?"

"Nothing," I snap. I'm so sick of her being in control of my life. "Can you just mind your own damn business for once?"

Her eyes widen. "Excuse me? This is our grandmother's and now *our* coven's Moon Room in an apothecary shop that we now *both* own. So yeah, this is also *my* damn business."

"Yes, but what I do isn't." And with that, I take a final glance at the mess I've made and begin to walk away. I don't care anymore.

"Quit being such a bitch and come clean this up," she yells.

"No," I say before flipping my hair over my shoulder.

Her jaw drops for a second before her eyebrows furrow. "I can't believe you're acting like this. I'm sure you'll come crying back to me soon enough when you need help with something."

I exhale when I reach the shop. I can't remember what I'm looking for or why I'm looking for it, but I feel the need to find it within me.

Without another thought, I leave the shop and my sister behind.

Seriously, where is this damn thing? I ask myself as I rummage through Granny Lizzie's bedroom for the sixth time this hour. I desperately need to find this crystal. I had the strongest urge to find it after I came back from Vik's after dinner.

I know this crystal will help me feel better. I can feel it in my bones. I'll do whatever it takes to locate it.

I pull open one of the tiny drawers of her jewelry box and spot a translucent crystal.

After releasing a sigh of relief, I hear a knock on the door. *Ugh, who the hell can that be?*

I quickly pocket the crystal and slam the drawer shut before making my way to the front door.

Once again, it's Joey. "You again? Seriously?" I ask.

He releases a sigh. "Yeah, Zar. It's me. Can I come in?"

"No," I say, ready to slam the door in his face.

"I brought your favorite wine," he says holding up a bottle of Syrah.

I cross my arms in front of me. "That's not my favorite anymore. In fact, I'm more of a gin and tonic girl these days," I say.

"Oh, all right. I didn't know. I'm sorry."

"Whatever," I tell him.

He sighs. "Well, here's the wine," he says as he hands me the bottle. "I just came to check on you. Make sure you're okay."

"Yup, I'm fine."

"Okay, that's good. See ya around, I guess," he says, turning to head back to his truck.

I glance around to make sure no one else is in the driveway. "Wait, Joey. I could use your help with something."

He turns around and raises a curious eyebrow at me. "Yeah?"

"Can you help me find a bat?" I ask.

Joey lets out a loud laugh. "A what? Did you just say a bat? Like a winged bat?"

I nod. "Yeah, what's so funny?"

"Oh, you're serious?" His large brown eyes stare at me. "What the hell do you want a bat for?"

"I—I just want to see one is all. Please."

He blows out a breath and shrugs. "I guess we can go to this one park that I pass on my way to work. They're usually lurking in the trees around there."

"Let's do it," I say, grabbing my keys off the table. "You're driving," I tell him before closing and locking the door behind me.

It doesn't take long for us to arrive at the park. I slam his truck door behind me once he parks, feeling determined to go and get this bat.

"Okay, where are the bats?" I ask.

"You just want to see one, right?" he asks.

I nod.

"All righty, then," he says, waving me along behind him. "Right this way."

We walk around the park for a few minutes before he stops in front of me. "I see some. Sleeping up in that tree."

"How do we get one down?" I ask.

"What? Are you crazy?" he retorts.

I wave him off before attempting to climb the tree. I shift my body and feel the selenite in my pocket, feeling better that it's still with me. One foot up, I swing my other up to climb higher, but it slips on some of the bark, causing me to fall back on the ground. Right on my ass.

Joey rushes over to me, eyes inspecting my body for signs of injury. "Zar, are you all right? You hurt?"

"I'm fine." Glancing down, I notice a small cut on my leg. I put my hand against it to stop it from bleeding. "Damn it."

"Here," Joey says before taking his shirt off and handing it over to me.

I roll my eyes. "You serious? It's a tiny cut. I'm fine."

"If you say so." He puts his shirt back on.

Placing my palms on the ground, I start to lift myself up when I spot a dead bat lying on the ground near the base of the tree, in between two giant roots.

"There's what I need." I stand up and walk over to the bat, scooping it up.

"Wait—you wanted a *dead* bat? I like you, Zara, but this isn't you. What the hell is going on with you?"

"Can you please leave me alone?" I snap. "I'm trying to put together a special potion for Luna, if you must know," I lie.

"Whatever you say," he says. "Well, you got what you wanted, I guess. Can we at least get you back home now?"

"Yup. I'm ready," I say, cupping the bat's small body in my hand. *All I need is a frog leg and a few other things, and I can finally start the potion.*

Joey drives me home and we exchange the fastest goodbyes possible. When I head into the house, I realize that I should probably hide the bat and a few of the other ingredients tonight until my shift tomorrow. That way, I can hide everything in the Workshop and work on my potions when needed. It's so exciting to think that I'm only one night's sleep away from finally bringing this plan to fruition.

The next morning, I arrive at the shop with the ingredients, determined to get this done. I briefly stash them in the Workshop before I start up the registers and get the shop prepared to open for the day.

Once everything is ready, I wait for over an hour but no one comes in. I figure this is the best opportunity I'll have to start working on the potions, so I switch our sign on the front door to Closed. As I do, I go over the list in my head to make sure I've got everything I need: St. John's wort, check; sage, check; a frog leg, check; peppermint oil, check; a bat's wing, check; and Granny Lizzie's selenite crystal, check.

When I walk into the Workshop, I grab all the necessary ingredients and place them into the cauldron one at a time, but when it's time to put the crystal in, I hesitate for a second. It feels *too* special to add to this potion. The room begins to spin and my eyesight blurs. It's like I'm drunk again, so I steady myself on the counter near the cauldron.

Focus on the mission, I think to myself before dropping the selenite into the cauldron. A puff of dark gray smoke forms a cloud above it and the crystal rises above the cauldron with it. I watch in awe as a bright light forms in the crystal for only a second before it turns dark and descends back down.

Success.

Feeling satisfied, I grab a few bottles and set them on the Workshop table. I decide to set the mood and with a flick of my hands, all the candles in the room are lit.

"Perfect," I say.

I make my way over to one of our other cauldrons, ready to start on the next potion. I wipe away a bead of sweat on my forehead before reaching for the herbs and oils I've set aside for this one.

"Time to move on to the final step," I whisper. This potion is a very simple recipe and I finally get the chance to use the two darker ingredients. When I find them exactly where I left them—tucked away in the corner of a shelf in the Workshop—I clasp my hands together in excitement.

"Yes! The moment I've been waiting for," I exclaim, though no one is around to hear my giddiness. I add in a slightly evil giggle for dramatic effect before grabbing the wolfsbane and hemlock.

I add in the majority of the ingredients, saving the two most important ones for last. I give the mixture a final forceful stir before reaching for the final herbs when Binxi hops up on the counter and looks at me.

He starts to paw at the bottles of the potion on the counter.

"Don't you dare," I say to Binxi. But it's too late. The glass bottles shatter the second they hit the floor, spilling all of the potion.

"Binxi, how could you?!" I cry out to him.

He turns his back to me.

"Oh, now you're gonna be like this? Traitor." I scoff and search for a roll of paper towels to clean up the spilled potion. But Binxi meows loudly, causing me to turn around. My eyes widen as his tail twitches right near a lit candle.

"Nooooo," I yell as the candle falls to the floor and sets the potion aflame.

I scream as it explodes. Smoke fills the room and a high-pitched noise rings in my ears before I collapse. The room goes black.

After a moment, my eyes shoot open. The smoke dissipates. I sit up and cough, spotting the bottles of poison on the counter near the cauldron. I blow out a breath when it hits me.

Oh, fuck. What have I done?

TWELVE

I'm not supposed to go into the shop today. It's Zara's shift today after all, and as sad as it makes me, we've been staying away from each other after our big blowout. She's been acting so strange and still wants nothing to do with me. Not to mention that she left me with a big mess to clean up. I don't know what the hell is going on with her, but I'm hoping that it's just stress or a phase or *something* and she goes back to being the sister I know and love soon.

As I'm planning out my laid-back day where I don't have to walk on eggshells around the house, I get a text from Gwyn.

> Hey, I just did inventory last night and we're running out of almost all the potions. Are you planning on making more?

Fuck. I'm usually so on top of that, but I haven't felt like myself with everything going on lately. They've also been selling like hot-cakes.

> I'll go in and make them today. Should I make more than normal? I feel like we're running out more quickly than we usually do.

> *Yes. I would double it. I think people are starting to get wind of us and the shop. It's good, but I'll need to keep a close eye on inventory for ordering.*

> *Okay. Thanks, babycakes.*

> *Sure thing, honeybuns. Xx*

It's so cheesy and cliché, but I can't help the way my heart soars and my stomach swoops. That is, until I remember that I have to go into the shop and see my sister. Said stomach drops like a rock. I sigh, but get all my shit together and head over.

As I pull up, I notice the sign is switched to Closed. Oh, Goddess. What now? I curse when I find the door locked as well.

I'm just setting my things down in the office when I hear a crash coming from the Workshop, followed by a scream. I drop everything and run.

I burst through the door to find a frazzled-looking Zara on the ground with her bangs singed, a satisfied-looking Binxi, and a huge mess on the counter and floor consisting of broken glass and spilled potions and ingredients, some of which are still sizzling and smoking.

Zara looks at me with panic in her eyes, but also *clarity*. It's the first time I've seen her look like herself in a while.

"Zara? What happened?" I ask, helping her to her feet.

"Luna! Thank the Three-Faced Goddess. I need your help."

"What is it? What's wrong? Are you okay?"

"I'm uninjured if that's what you're asking, but I just had an accident and it basically woke me up from this trance I've been in."

My blood turns to ice. "Trance?"

She nods, pale as snow. "Yes. I don't know who put it on me or how it happened, but I just tried to make a potion to poison us," she says, gesturing to the mess in front of her. My eyes widen in shock as I spot the hemlock and the wolfsbane. *Shit.*

"Thankfully, Binxi sabotaged it and one of the ingredients caught fire and jolted me out of it. I don't know how long this reprieve will last though. You can't let me mess up anything more than I already have. I think I did something else before this too, but I don't know what exactly. It's something to do with this crystal." She pulls it out of the spare cauldron.

She's on the verge of tears and panic laces her tone. I walk up to her and pull her into my arms. Even though this is bad news bears, I'm so relieved to have my *sister* looking back at me.

"It's okay, Zar. Don't worry, we're going to figure this out."

She sighs in such relief in my arms. I hate that she's been in a fucking *trance* and I wasn't able to help her. I mean, I knew she was acting strangely, but I thought she was just so mad at me that it was affecting our relationship. I never dreamed that it could be something so much more serious.

She pulls back and I see tears in her eyes. "How are we going to fix this?"

"First things first. You text the coven group chat and have them meet us here ASAP. I will look through the spell book and see what I can find."

She nods, grabbing her phone. I keep half an eye on her as I flip through the book. I know she's herself now, but we have no idea for how long. Eventually I find what I'm looking for. A purification spell. I'll need the assistance of the entire coven, including all of their blood and a good portion of Zara's. I don't like that, and I know she won't either, but at this point we need to do whatever we have to in order to remove whatever is on her. If we knew *what* it was, or even *who* was behind it, we could maybe go a different route, but with things being the way they are, this is our best bet.

"They'll be here in an hour," Zara tells me.

"Perfect. That'll give me time to cleanse the Moon Room and get everything together that we'll need."

"What do you need me to do?"

I glance at her, feeling uncertain.

"Well, Zar, as much as I would love your assistance, I'm hesitant to have you help."

Her face falls but she nods. She knows that this is too important, and if she's still under someone else's influence, it would be too dangerous to have her contribute in any way.

Luckily, Gwyn shows up with Joey minutes after, and I have Joey keep an eye on Zara while Gwyn and I get everything prepared. I look over at my sister through the whole process, and I'm glad to see that Joey seems to be entertaining her. It's the first time I've seen her smile in a while, and the sight lifts something in my chest.

Gwyn and I go down to the Moon Room and smudge the space. More so than we've ever done before, making sure to get every nook and cranny. When we've gone through with sage, palo santo, and sweet grass, we pour a circle of sacred salts in the center of the room, right underneath the magic skylight where the full moon is pouring light into the space. We got lucky with timing. This spell is best done under a full moon, and I'm grateful that we don't have to wait for the next one.

Once that's all done, I return to the Workshop and make the potion we will need. By this time, the rest of the coven has shown up. I had Allegra bring me a bowl of sea water. It will be the base of the potion, and it's particularly effective for cleansing. Once it's boiling, I add in more salts, rose petals, sage, and mint. When that's ready, I call the coven into the Workshop. They each add three drops of their blood to represent the three faces of our beloved Goddess. I add mine, and finally, Zara adds hers last. She adds nine instead, and I hate that she'll have to spill even more before the night is over.

I stir the potion again, mixing everything together and finally pouring my color magic into it. When it's finished, it glows softly, radiating a peaceful feeling that seems to seep into the air around us. Zara breathes a soft sigh of relief and I haven't even done anything to her yet. It makes me confident in the outcome.

"Okay, everything's ready. Let's go down to the Moon Room."

I grab the potion and head down first, the other girls after me. Joey follows even though he won't be able to participate. As long as he stays out of the circle, everything will be fine. I'm grateful for his presence when Zara starts attempting to escape. I was wondering when the mysterious influence would return. It seems it finally has, with a vengeance. Watching my sister scream and thrash as we have to physically force her into the center of the circle breaks my heart, and a tear rolls down my cheek. Joey sets her down in a chair in the center of the room and the salt, luckily without disturbing anything. The other witches immobilize her with their magic. I know we're doing the right thing and that this isn't actually her fighting back, but it's difficult to process that at the moment. It feels like I'm torturing her instead of helping her.

I grab my special ceremonial rune-covered bowl and walk to the center with her. Joey moves to the edge of the room, making sure to stay out of the way. With a flick of my wrist, I light the candles, and the soft glow illuminates my sister's features. It's her, but not. I can see clearly now that there's something, or should I say some*one* occupying her space.

I look into her eyes. "You will fucking leave my sister *alone.*"

The thing inside her chuckles darkly. "You can't make me leave."

"Watch me, motherfucker."

With that, I grab my knife and slash her palm open. She cries out in pain, but now that I've seen the *thing* inside of her, it's easier. I hold the bowl underneath her palm, letting her blood pool inside.

I start chanting, low and deep, and the others join me. Zara starts screaming in earnest and her blood is almost black. We keep chanting until her blood turns the normal red color it should be. Zara sags in her seat and we finally stop speaking. I set the bowl off to the side and grab the potion. I dump it over her head and the moment it connects with her skin, she sighs in relief.

"Is it over?" she asks, sounding more herself than she has in a while, despite the exhaustion coating her words.

"Almost, Zar. The last thing we have to do is bring this outside and burn it," I say, gesturing to her tainted blood.

We release her from our magic and she stands on shaky legs. Joey helps her now that we've broken the circle. He rushes to her, grabbing her hand and supporting her with a hand on her low back. She smiles gratefully at him and we all make our way slowly up the stairs and outside.

I pour alcohol into the bowl with her blood, which will allow us to set fire to it. Before beginning the cleansing, I had Hazel and Morgan get the fire set up. Joey lights it now, and when it's hot enough, we begin chanting again, forming a circle around the flames. A horrible screeching noise is coming from the bowl, as if whoever was controlling her is screaming in pain and protest.

I hand the bowl to my sister, and she takes it with shaking hands. I worry for a second that she's going to drop it, but resolve hardens her features. When our chanting reaches its pinnacle, she tosses the blood and alcohol into the flames. There's a *whoosh* as it connects, and then the scent of rotten burning flesh permeates the air. We all wrinkle our noses, but Zara sags beside me. Joey rushes forward to catch her.

"I think it's time we get you home, huh, sis?" I ask.

She turns and gives me a relieved smile and a nod of her head.

"Actually," Nora pipes in before we can leave. "I want to see the crystal you were telling us about. The one that Zara used in the other potion."

I see the exhaustion on Zara's face and almost tell Nora that it can wait, but after everything that's happened, we really need to be extra vigilant.

"Let's go, then," Zara says, clearly on the same wavelength as me.

We head to the Workshop to see it lying unassumingly on the counter. It's a rock cluster with mostly clear stone. There's some areas where it's almost brown or dark pink.

"What is it, Nora?" I ask.

"Selenite. It's mainly used for protection and healing." She carefully picks it up, and immediately gasps upon holding it. "There's something different about this one. It feels strange. Like it used to hold something more but now it's empty."

"Can I see it?" I ask, holding out my hands for it. I can tell what she means. Instead of bolstering me like normal stones do, there's only a void.

"I have a vague recollection of it lighting up when I would hold it before I used the potion on it. There was also a comforting feeling about it before. I don't get that same sense from it anymore," Zara chimes in.

Gwyn takes it from me and gasps. She's having a vision.

When she comes out of it, she stares at the stone. "It was a protection spell for the two of you. Granny Lizzie keyed it specifically for you both. You took the spell off of it, Zara."

My sister flinches at her words, and I give Gwyn a warning glare. I know she's not trying to hurt her, but Zara doesn't need this right now. Gwyn gives me an apologetic look.

"We can deal with all of this another time. I really need to get Zara to bed."

The girls and Joey all nod, giving hugs before taking off.

I'm finally able to take my sister home, Binxi in tow. It's been a long, stressful day, and not only am I starving, but I'm exhausted and relieved all at the same time. I can only imagine how Zara's feeling.

We walk through the door to our house, and I hear her sigh in contentment. I smile softly to myself. I don't know what it is about this house, but it almost feels alive. Like a dear friend that greets and welcomes us whenever we enter. I can tell Zara feels the same.

"Hungry?" I ask.

She nods. "Starving. I feel as if I haven't eaten in days."

I wonder if that's indeed true. If whoever's influence she was under wanted her harmed, making her starve herself would definitely aid in that mission. Or at least weaken her.

I head to the kitchen, pouring us each a much-needed glass of red wine. We each take a sip, and I instantly feel myself relax.

"What sounds good?"

"Tacos."

I smirk. I knew it. This bitch loves Mexican food, but tacos are her absolute favorite.

"Coming right up."

I take out everything I need and get the meat started. While that's cooking, I make my famous pico. It doesn't take long before everything is finished, and I pile the meat and pico as well as cheese, refried beans, sour cream, and an avocado onto a tortilla.

I hand it over to Zara and she inhales it. In fact, I've *never* seen her eat so quickly. She finishes it in record time, and I get out some tortilla chips for her to dip in the salsa.

It takes longer for mine to disappear, but when we both have full bellies and a pleasant buzz going from the wine, I really look at her. She has bags under haunted eyes, and I beat myself up for not noticing what was going on sooner. I'm her *sister*. I should've known that something was up.

"How are you?" I ask, although I mentally slap myself for how stupid of a question that is.

"I'll be okay," she says, not actually answering my question.

"I know you will. But you don't have to be strong for anyone right now. It's just me. So tell me really. How are you?"

She takes a deep shuddering breath. "I'm...terrible, honestly. I don't know who I can trust right now. I don't even know if I can trust myself because I don't know if my poor judgment is what got me into this situation in the first place. On top of that, pieces are missing from my memories. Like I have vague pictures of some stuff, but I feel like there is so much that's just absent. It worries me, and I have no idea what else I was made to do during that time. What if..." She trails off, choking up.

"What, Zar?" I ask gently.

"What if I did something horrible?" she whispers so quietly I'm barely able to hear her.

Without another word, I pull her into my arms. She breaks down in my embrace, and I let her get all of her emotions out while I figure out what to say to her. She finally quiets and I pull back to look at her. She won't meet my gaze.

"Look at me." She still doesn't. "*Look at me, Zara.*"

She finally meets my eyes and I can see every emotion she's feeling. She's worried I'm going to judge her. Little does she know, she could do pretty much anything and I wouldn't bat an eye. She's been the person I've cared about most for my entire life, and I will have her back no matter what. I let all of that shine through my own eyes before I speak.

"If you *did* do something horrible, it wasn't *you*. I know you, Zara. You wouldn't hurt a fly. You have a good heart and you're a wonderful person. This isn't your fault. Whatever was done is on the person that hexed you. No one else."

She breaks down again, my words seeming to unravel something inside her. This time she doesn't cry for nearly as long, and when she breaks away from me, I'm relieved to see that she looks more like herself. Exhausted and stressed and all of the things, but at least she seems more unburdened.

"Come on, babes. Let's get you to bed."

While she heads to the bathroom to do her nightly routine, I make her a sleeping draft. I don't know if she'll even need it with how tired she is, but I want her to have a healing dreamless sleep.

I take it to her bedroom just as she enters in her nightgown. She sits on her bed, and I give her the tea.

"Drink all of this before you go to sleep, okay?"

She nods. It's not the first time I've made this particular concoction for her.

"Do you need anything else?"

"Binxi."

I smile. I'm about to go fetch him when he meows and hops onto the bed as if he was able to sense her need for him.

"It's hard to believe this is actually Chad."

I suck in a sharp breath. We haven't talked about this since our big blowout.

"Are you still upset with me about it?"

She shakes her head. "I know you were only doing it out of love and to protect me. You're always there for me, Lu. And I have to admit, not only does he deserve it, but he's much more pleasant this way."

I let out a surprised chuckle. "I thought so too. Go to sleep, sister. I'll see you in the morning."

I close the door behind me and head to my own room. I lie in bed, unable to fall asleep as I try to figure out who harmed my sister. Crone help them when I find them because I will make them *pay.*

The next morning I wake early and get some breakfast going. I want Zara to have a nice meal when she wakes up, along with some fancy sweet-as-shit coffee. She comes down soon after I get the French toast on the stove, just like I knew she would. She can never resist breakfast and coffee, and I was sure the smells would entice her from sleep.

She ambles down, looking a little worse for wear, and I chuckle, immediately handing her some caffeine. She takes a greedy drink, plopping down on a bar stool.

After a few minutes, she starts to come out of her zombie-like state. We chat as I continue making our meal, but she seems distracted, looking at her phone every few minutes.

"What is it?" I ask.

She sighs. "Nothing. I just texted Vik last night and I was hoping he would've responded by now."

"Well, it is his turn to open the shop this morning. He's probably just busy."

She nods, but I can see the disappointment on her face.

I finish making our meal and we eat in comfortable silence. It seems we're both starving after the events of the last two days. I think as I eat, and I have an idea that I have a good feeling about. I want to cheer Zara up, and even though I want to spend time with her now that she's back to herself, I can see that she also wants the comfort of the man in her life. And as much as I want to be the only person she needs, I know that's not realistic. It's a good thing that she has multiple people in her corner who care for her.

"How about this," I propose. "I'll get ready and go relieve Vik from his shop duties today, and send him over here to hang out with you."

Her eyes light up. "Really? You wouldn't mind? I'd love to see him."

"Of course I don't mind. Let me change and put my face on and then I'll head out. The shop is already opened for the day so I shouldn't have much to do anyway." I still don't like the guy, but he makes Zara happy and that's all I care about.

She smiles. "Thanks so much, Lu. You really are the best sister a girl could ask for."

"I know," I tell her with a wink before heading upstairs.

Half an hour later, I'm pulling up to Enchanted Elixirs. I roll my eyes—looks as though Vik forgot to turn the sign to Open. I make my way to the front door and notice that the shop looks darker than normal. I pull on the door but it doesn't budge. This isn't looking good.

I unlock the door and enter. "Hello?" No answer. "Vik?"

Nothing. Fucker forgot to show up for his shift. I turn everything on and open the shop before reaching for my phone and calling him. I'm going to lay into his ass and then I'm going to make him go comfort my sister.

The only problem is that he isn't answering his phone. I leave him a pissed-off message, then text him, then call him again. Nothing. I huff right as the door chimes. I turn to find a customer entering. I smile, welcoming them in, and while they look around, I text Zara that Vik is MIA.

THIRTEEN

Zara

I'm vegging out on the couch in our living room when my phone vibrates on the coffee table. I reach for it and see a message from Luna.

> Hey, have you heard from Vik? I think he's MIA. He's not at the shop and I can't get ahold of him.

I quickly type back that I'm going to call him. When I do, it goes straight to his voicemail. I try to recall our last conversation. *Where could he be?*

I decide to text the coven group chat to ask if anyone has seen Viktor at all lately. Everyone replies with a resounding no, but Allegra says she is running errands around town and will keep an eye out. I thank her and lean back on the couch, releasing a loud sigh. I wonder if I should call him again, but it does feel pointless since it went straight to his voicemail. Ugh.

When I close my eyes to rest, my phone starts to ring. They spring open and I lunge forward to check the name on the screen. Morgan.

I let out a small sigh in disappointment before answering. "Hello?"

"Hey, Zar, I'm sorry to hear Vik is MIA. Want some company?" she asks.

I glance around the empty room, contemplating if I'd rather be alone right now. I feel a little freaked that Vik is suddenly gone, so I go with my gut. "I'd love some, actually. Can you come over?"

"Yeah, I'm with Hazel now. We're on our way. See you soon, girl."

"Thanks, love. See you both soon," I say before ending the call. I smile. It does feel really nice to have girlfriends in my corner who aren't just Luna. We've always had each other, and while our sisterly bond is awesome, having close friends who feel like sisters is really nice too.

I head into the kitchen to prepare some snacks and wine for their arrival. It's early, but I figure if another guy is deciding to dump or ghost me, I'd better be prepared. Although, I am worried that something bad has happened to Vik. Something in my gut feels really off, but I'm not sure what to think of it.

As I finishing cutting up some peppers for hummus, there's a knock on the door. I toss the knife in the sink and head to the door. When I open it, I'm surprised to see both girls each holding a bottle of wine.

"Hi, Zar. We came prepared," Hazel says.

I let out a laugh. "I'd say so." I hold the door open for them as they enter. "Thanks so much for coming by, girls. Luna was trying to give me and Vik some alone time, so she went to the shop to relieve him of his shift, and he's not even there."

"Asshole," Hazel says.

Morgan gives her a look before turning to me. "Wait, are we calling him an asshole, or we don't know yet?"

I shake my head. "We don't know yet. I do feel like something is wrong, but I can't put my finger on it. I keep running into this woman who gives me the creeps, but aside from that, the only thing I can think of is that whoever is taking these witches may have taken Vik too."

"Oh, that's interesting," Morgan says. "But why would they take a guy? He's not a witch or even in the coven."

I process her words for a minute. "Yeah, that's a good point. I guess I just assumed maybe it was a way to get us witches at the shop angered. Or to give us a warning of some kind."

"Yeah, after my friend going missing, and now this, who knows what the hell is going on. It is really scary," Morgan says.

Hazel nods. "Yeah, it really is."

We all jump a bit when my phone starts vibrating loudly on the coffee table. I run over to grab it. Vik's name flashes across the screen. "It's Vik," I tell them.

"Answer!" Nora says.

I swipe to accept the call and answer with a calm "Hello?"

"Zara. It's Viktor." His tone sounds off. Almost standoffish.

"Yeah, I know. Is everything okay? Luna said you didn't show up for your shift and I've been worried sick." There's silence on the other end. "Vik, you there?"

He clears his throat. "Yeah, I'm here." He sighs. "Zara, you've been acting so differently lately, and I just feel like you're not the same woman as when we first met."

"I'm not any different. Well, I guess I sort of was. I don't know. I'm still trying to figure out exactly what happened, but I promise I'm still me."

"Hm."

I wait for him to say more, but he doesn't. "Hello?"

"I don't know what to say," he says. His words begin to anger me.

"You don't even realize what I've been through lately, Vik." He doesn't know about the explosion in the Workshop, or whatever spell I was under; he didn't even show up for his shift.

"Just because you've been going through something doesn't give you the right to be a bitch."

His words seal his fate. I let Chad walk all over me, and I can't continue to let this happen.

"Oh, I'm a bitch, huh? In that case, let me do you a favor. We're done, Viktor. Oh and by the way, you're fired. Have a nice life," I say firmly before ending the call. When I look up to Morgan and Hazel, they're staring at me with wide eyes.

"What just happened?" Morgan asks.

"Turns out we *are* calling him an asshole now," I say. "He doesn't believe me and barely had anything to say. *And* had the audacity to call me a bitch." I toss my phone on the couch. "Whatever. I'm done letting guys take advantage of me like this. He doesn't even know all the crazy shit I've just been put through." Tears begin to roll down my cheeks.

Morgan runs over to me as Hazel searches for a box of tissues. "Oh, honey," Morgan says, embracing me in a big bear hug. "Forget him. He's not worth any tears. No guy is."

I nod and hug her back. When I pull away, Hazel is there rubbing my back with one hand and offering me a tissue with the other. I take it and dab at the tears. "Thank you," I say, looking at both of them. "I'm so glad you both are here. It means more than you know."

"Anytime, babe. We're here for you and any of our sisters. Always." Hazel hands me one more tissue.

I take a few deep breaths. "Love you both. So, how about that wine?"

They exchange a quick glance. "Girl, sit down. I'm on it," Morgan says before making her way into the kitchen.

"Thanks," I say, plopping back down on the couch. Hazel sits down next to me.

"What else can we do to help?" she asks.

I shrug. "Let's just chill for a while."

"You got it," Morgan says, handing me my glass of wine.

I take a sip before asking, "All right, enough about me and this drama. What's new with you both?"

The girls laugh and we all chat for the next few hours. We're interrupted when Luna calls me.

"Hey, girl, just done with my shift and checking in," she says.

"Everything is going great," I say. "The first update is that I broke it off with Vik."

She gasps. "No way!"

"Yes way! He didn't show up for his shift, didn't answer calls, and then had the nerve to tell me I've been acting different and being a bitch. Which, we both know I have, but screw him. He didn't even believe me. I'm so sick of letting guys treat me like shit."

"Zar, holy shit, I'm so proud of you." The excitement and pride in her voice radiates through the phone.

"Thanks. I'm feeling proud of me too." I look over at the girls and say, "Oh, and Hazel and Morgan have been keeping me company. I think they're probably gonna head out soon though, since it's getting late."

"Oh, glad to hear that you've had some company since I ended up having to work today thanks to that douchebag." She lets out a loud sigh. "Okay. Well, if they're leaving, I don't want you to be all alone tonight."

I hear the hesitation in her words. "Shit, that's right. You wanted to spend the night at Gwyn's, didn't you?"

"Guilty," she admits. "But I totally won't if you need me. You know what? I better not. You need me more and she'll understand."

No matter how many fights we have, she never hesitates to step in as my protector and older sister. "Lu, I appreciate it, but I promise I'll be fine by myself. In fact, I think I have somewhere I need to go tonight anyway. A certain someone I need to apologize to."

"Go get him, bitch. Love you," she says.

"Love you too," I say. We end the call and I fill the girls in on how I left things with Joey.

"You need to go. Now. Go get him. He's been smitten with you since the first day y'all met," Morgan says.

"Yeah, I'm not sure he's gonna get past the whole dead bat thing," I say and shake my head. "I'm so embarrassed."

"Only one way to find out," Hazel says.

When I arrive at Joey's, my heart starts to race. I fidget with the hem of my yellow dress, debating if a dress was the right move. More importantly, what if he doesn't want anything to do with me?

Ignoring my nerves, I knock on the door. Joey slowly opens it and stares at me. "Zara? What are you doing here?"

"Hi," I say. "I, uh—can I come in? I have a lot to tell you."

He stands motionless, only his eyes scanning me. I sense his hesitation, not that I blame him one bit. "Don't worry, my days of picking up dead bats—or any bats, really—are done. Promise."

He chuckles nervously before opening the door all the way. When I enter, he stands back as though I'm about to bite. He closes the door behind me before leading the way over to the living room. He sits in the middle of his couch, so I sit in a nearby recliner. He already seems like he's keeping his distance, so I choose to play it safe and not make him feel uncomfortable.

"So, if you're not here to take me on any more dead bat adventures, what are you here for?" he asks. I cringe slightly at his direct tone, but I get it. He senses my tension and his face softens. "Sorry, I know you've been through a lot lately. I'm still me though. Still here for you."

I sigh. "Thank you."

"Always," he says with a smile, and I'm instantly comforted by the way he makes me feel. "Wait, before you do. Want a gin and tonic?"

"Ew, absolutely not," I say. "But I'd love a drink. Have any wine?"

He smiles. "There's the Zara I remember. Let me go grab a bottle of your favorite red." My cheeks redden at his words.

When he returns with the bottle and two glasses of Syrah, I switch over to the couch to get comfortable.

"This okay?" I ask.

He nods and takes his seat right next to me. I spend the next several minutes telling him about my breakup with Vik. "Mostly though, I came to tell you that I remember you telling me you had feelings for me after you and Tiffany broke up."

He nods.

I rest my hand on his shoulder. "I have feelings for you too."

"You do?" he asks.

I nod and smile. "I do." I sit up straight before I add, "But look, I understand if you don't want much to do with me anymore thanks to everything that happened, but I had to tell you my true feelings and apologize for hurting you. I really didn't mean to..."

"I have to admit, I was crushed when I came by to tell you my feelings for you. I respected that you were with Vik, but I just had this bad vibe about him. And then you started acting so differently that it scared me. Which now I know wasn't your fault." He clears his throat. "But, I could tell you weren't yourself. I wanted to help you, but I didn't know how."

A tear makes its way down my cheek. "I'm so sorry."

He leans forward and wipes away my tear with his thumb. Our eyes meet, and I want to melt right then and there. My breath hitches when I notice his eyes on my lips.

"I've wanted you all along. I wish I had told you sooner, but when I found out you had a girlfriend, I knew I couldn't—"

He presses his lips against mine. His hand makes its way into my hair as he kisses me slowly and softly and I savor every second. I pull away and we exchange a smile.

"I've been wanting to do that for a very long time," he says.

I whimper and pull him in for another kiss. I brush my fingers through his hair and he kisses me harder, biting my lower lip. His hand softly wraps around my neck before making its way down to my breasts. Pulling down my bra with his hand, he kisses them before taking a nipple in his mouth. Warmth and wetness form between my thighs. "I need you, Joey."

"I'm all yours, Zar," he says, lifting up my dress and climbing on top of me. Kissing my body, he pushes my dress up over my head and he moans at the sight of me in just my bra and panties. He kisses me harder and slowly moves his lips to my neck and chest. One hand grabbing the back of my head, slightly tugging my hair, and the other in my bra, cupping my breast and flicking my nipple. I let out a soft moan and arch my back on the couch, allowing his hand to find the hook of my bra. He unlatches it, and I take it off. Joey lets out a chuckle when I toss it swiftly to the floor.

I bite my lower lip and begin lifting up his shirt, dying to get it off. His arm reaches behind his back and he pulls it up over his head, revealing his bare chest. I touch him, my fingers slowly inching their way down to his jeans. When I'm there, I feel his hard bulge through them and a small burst of slickness hits me.

I eagerly attempt to unbuckle his belt, but I'm struggling.

"I got it," he assures me as he quickly removes his belt and lets his pants hit the floor.

"I could've just used my magic to remove them," I say.

He laughs. "This already feels magical just the way it is."

I whimper and lean forward, grabbing hold of his boxers. I pull them down, releasing his cock. My eyes widen at its size. My stare is interrupted when his finger tilts my chin up so that my eyes meet his instead.

"You like what you see?" he asks, smirking, and I quiver. I've never wanted someone in this way before. And wanted them so. Damn. Much. I wrap my hand around his cock and bring my mouth to the tip. I use my tongue to slowly tease him before taking him fully in my mouth.

"Oh shit," he says as he slowly yanks my hair back and forth and my mouth follows suit. I suck him for a few minutes before he pulls out, lowering himself and kissing me. His hand slowly makes its way down between my thighs. He moves my thong to the side, and his finger quickly finds my clit. I'm ready to explode.

"Fuck, baby. So wet for me." His finger is moving up and down, flicking my clit, teasing me until I'm just about to come. My legs begin to shake and he kisses my mouth harder, stifling the sound of my pleasure.

My orgasm crests through me and when I'm finally boneless, he kisses me one more time before pulling down my underwear and tossing them on the floor. I lie on the couch as he wraps my legs around his torso before swooping me up and carrying me to his bedroom.

When we make it to the bed, he lays me down, teasing my entire body with his mouth until his tongue meets my clit. He licks me passionately before his fingers begin to work their magic too. I watch as he kisses, sucks, and fingers me until I come again, completely soaking his mouth and chin.

His eyes meet mine as he climbs on top of me. There's a desire in his eyes I've never seen before, and it brings another rush between my legs.

I pause for a moment to ask, "Wait, I'm clean, by the way. Are you?"

He nods. "I was tested right after Tiffany. Never could trust her." I nod, trying to pull him forward back into the moment. He kisses me once before pulling away again to ask, "Shit. Should I go grab a condom?"

"I'm on birth control, and I definitely don't want anything between us."

"Oh, fuck yes," he says as he places my hands above my head, holding them down as his cock brushes against my clit, teasing me once again. It makes me so hot that he's having his wicked way with me.

I gasp. "Please," I beg. "Fuck me."

At my words, his hard cock enters me. We both let out a moan. My legs wrap around him and my pussy pulses with each throb of his dick inside me.

He fucks me slowly before speeding up. I can tell he's about to come, and my legs are shaking beneath us as we both climax in sync with each other.

When we finish, his mouth meets mine again and he kisses me hard before rolling over. His body next to mine, I put my hand and head on his chest, looking up at him, and feeling the best I've felt in a long time.

"Can you believe we've already been together for a few weeks now?" I ask, looking over my agenda on my phone for the week.

He nods before kissing my forehead. "These have been the best few weeks of my life."

My lips curve up into a big, cheesy grin. I feel so relaxed and just like my true self when I'm around him. He flashes me a big smile back when my phone rings. It's Allegra.

Before I can even say hello, she speed talks into the phone. "Zara, another witch has gone missing. Oh my Mother, I can't believe this. What is happening? Another one of us. This is too mu—"

"Allegra, breathe," I say, trying to hide my own anxiety. "Are you absolutely sure?"

"Yes," she says emphatically. "I gotta go—Nora is calling me back, and I need to tell her the news."

I thank her for letting me know and tell her I love her before ending the call. I try to fight back the tears as I set my phone back on my nightstand. "Another witch is gone, Joey."

"What the hell is going on?" he says in response. "This is getting bad."

I nod. "I know, this is so damn scary."

He wraps his arms around me and squeezes. "You're okay, babe. I know I don't have magic, but I'll do anything in my power to protect you."

His words are calming and consoling.

"Thank you," I tell him. "Also, I'm pretty sure it's after eight. You better get going to work, mister. You're gonna be late."

He exhales loudly. "Shit, yeah. Let me get dressed and head out of here." He leans toward me, kissing my forehead again. I close my eyes, permitting my lips to form a hint of a smile.

I watch as Joey gets dressed and grabs his stuff. "Have a good day," I tell him.

"You too, my love," he says before giving me a see-you-later kiss.

The front door shuts and I decide it's probably time for me to get up for the day. Gwyn is working at the shop, so maybe Luna and I can get in some quality sister time since it's been a while.

My feet hit the floor and I stare at the wall for a moment. Some days, it takes me forever to get out of bed, but especially when I'm in my head about all these witches going missing. I sigh and see Binxi on the floor next to my nightstand.

"How you doin', my sweet Binxi boy?" I scoot closer to him and start to gently massage behind his ears. He purrs and gets to his feet, making his way over to me, rubbing his body against my legs and demanding more love.

Figuring it's easier, I kneel to the ground to give him all the love he needs. "You're such a good boy now, Chad." He meows and I giggle.

As I start to stand back up, I notice a crumpled-up piece of paper that Binxi must've been sitting on. I smirk. "Always finding some kind of paper or bag to lie on, huh, buddy?" I pick it up and recognize the handwriting immediately. It's a letter from Granny Lizzie.

Oh my dearest Luna and Zara,

I was hoping you'd never receive this letter, but it does appear my intuition was correct. If you are reading this now, it means that the mage, Viktor Drexel, has somehow returned to Salem and become close to one or both of you. He is very dangerous and deceptive. He's capable of finding out intricate details about your lives to become closer and appear trustworthy. Nevertheless, do not trust him.

If you are still in the house and have access to my room, I have a brown leather-bound journal in which you'll find more details. Specifically, please find the dried Epigaea repens, a Mayflower, which serves as a bookmark.

Please stay safe, my girls.

All my magical love,

Granny Lizzie

I toss the letter to my bed and race into Granny Lizzie's bedroom. It's still a bit of a disaster from me apparently ransacking it in search of the crystal. It hits me that there's a chance I destroyed it while under his spell. The moment I'm in her room, I rush to her nightstand. *It's got to be in here.*

I don't have to search long, finding it at the very bottom, peeking through the mess I made earlier. *Note to self: clean this room.* I really must've not been myself if I left it this messy. I love to keep things tidy and organized.

I toss a few things to the side and grab the journal. Surprisingly, it's dusty and a bit torn, but it's still intact, its weight a testament to the wisdom of my grandmother's words inside. Moving a few items off her bed, I plop down and open the journal. The first few entries are filled with her grief and fear of the witch trials. Shit, that means this is from the late seventeenth century. Damn. I close the journal and my eyes to rest my hand on it and exhale for a minute, taking it all in.

When I open it back up, I gently flip through it in search of the page with the dried flower bookmark, and I stop when I find it. Already, I can see Viktor's name mentioned several times.

I skim through the entry, noticing water marks—most likely tear stains—across the page. Reading her words, I can't believe I ever trusted Viktor. *How could I be so fucking stupid?* My eyes go large when I read her final words. I gasp and my hand flies to my mouth, the journal falling to the floor.

Holy Three-Faced Goddess, this isn't good.

My heart races as I head straight to Luna's room.

"Luna, you are never going to believe this shit," I shout, opening her door and searching her room. She's not here.

"Luna?" I call out around the house. "You home?"

I go to call her until I realize she probably spent the night at Gwyn's. But, Gwyn is working today. I calmly remind myself that Luna is probably with Gwyn at the shop, so I head back to my room to throw on an outfit.

As soon as I'm dressed, I grab my keys and phone, lock up, and drive to the shop. When I pull in, I see the Closed sign in the window. Before I panic, I swiftly walk up to the door. It's locked and no one is around. *Where is Gwyn? And where is Luna?*

My breath shortens and a sweat breaks out over my entire body as I head back to the car. *Seriously, where are they?* I fight back tears as I fumble to get my phone from the car. I try to call Luna, then Gwyn. No answer.

My thoughts begin to spiral. *What do I do? What can I do? How did this happen? Who can I call?* I blow out a breath and decide to call Joey since I know he'll calm me down.

"Hey, I'm freaking out a bit and trying not to. Have you seen Luna or Gwyn?"

"I haven't, why? What's going on?" he asks.

The tears start to pour. I feel like I can barely breathe.

"Deep breaths, Zar," he reminds me. "Take three for me."

I pause and follow his directions, taking three inhale-exhales. "Thanks, Joey. I needed that." I inhale slowly again. "But, I am scared. I don't know where they are. I have a feeling they're missing like the other witches. I need to go find them."

"Where are you? Let me come help you," he offers.

"I'm at the shop. Well, in my car out front," I say and glance around to the different stores and restaurants along the strip. My eyes stop at the bar that I was in the day Viktor came and comforted me.

"Okay, I'll leave work now and meet you there," Joey says, interrupting my thoughts.

"Wait," I say, still staring at the bar. "Don't come, actually."

"Huh? Zar, you okay? I don't mind helping."

"Joey, I know. And I love how much you help me, but I just realized that I really need to handle this on my own."

He sighs. "You sure? What if something bad happens to you though? I'm worried sick."

"I know you are. And truthfully, I am too. But..." I hesitate. "You have to trust me on this. I know I need to do this on my own."

"Okay," he says. "Be safe, and please call me if you change your mind. You know I'll be there in a second. Wherever you need me."

I smile. "I know, Joey. Thank you. And don't worry, I will. I'll call you back later when I can."

"You really are one strong, magical girl, Zara. The bravest one I know. Talk soon," he says before we end the call.

I start up the engine, feeling angered and determined. *What would Luna do?* I ask myself.

I decide to make one more phone call, and Morgan answers on the first ring. "Hey, Z, what's up?" she says.

"Hey," I say calmly. "Please call the coven and have everyone meet me in the Moon Room within the next hour. Luna and Gwyn are missing, but I'm pretty sure I know where they are."

We need to get to Vik's house immediately.

Fourteen

I wake slowly, enjoying the feeling of lounging in my girlfriend's bed. There's soft light spilling in through the window, and I'm so cozy I could stay here all day. Maybe I can convince Gwyn—I can be *very* convincing, if I do say so myself. Especially with my tongue.

I turn over, intending to do just that, but the bed next to me is empty, the sheets cool. I frown. This is putting a serious wrench in my "let's stay in bed all day" plan. It's not unusual for Gwyn to get up before me, however. She's an early bird. I usually try to get up with her, but I'm out of the habit. This is the first time I've slept over in weeks. I've been so concerned about Zara. Not only was she hexed and made to try to kill not only herself, but me as well, but she also had to break up with that asshat. Fucking Vik. If I ever see him again, I'm going to cut his balls off myself. And then maybe feed them to Binxi.

I roll out of bed, needing coffee if we're actually going to be getting up and doing productive adult things. I head to the bathroom first, seeing to my body's needs before brushing my teeth. Then I make my way to the kitchen. That's where Gwyn always is, I've noticed. She enjoys cooking, but she also finds comfort in the space with all the windows.

But she isn't there. I frown again. That's strange. I also can't smell any coffee. A pit forms in my stomach, and I take a few deep breaths to calm myself.

"Gwyn!" I yell, waiting anxiously for her reply. When I get nothing back I yell again, more hysterically this time. Still nothing. Panic starts rushing through me in earnest now as I quickly search the house. She's nowhere.

I look out front and see that her car is still here. My heart beats harder and my breaths come faster as I scramble for my phone. I call her and bite my lip as it rings.

"Please answer, baby."

My heart stops altogether when I hear it ringing in the kitchen. I follow the sound and find her phone sitting on the counter next to an attempt at preparing coffee. The bag is out and the carafe is full of water, but that's it. Dread pounds through my veins. Something is horribly wrong. It hits me then. The missing witches. They got to Gwyn. *Fuck.*

I have to find her. I throw on my clothes in a rush. I tuck my phone in my pocket, grab my keys, and take off for the shop. I have an idea of how I can find her.

It's early still—only 7:30. The shop won't open for another hour and a half. I'm grateful Gwyn lives right down the street because I don't have any patience. If she lived any farther I might've gotten into an accident for how fast I'm driving. When I arrive, my hands are shaking so bad that it takes me a full minute to unlock the fucking door. I'm cursing the whole time, and I'm sure if anyone were out and about right now, they would be looking at me like I was crazy.

I *finally* get the door open and rush to the Workshop. I thank the Crone that I had the foresight to hang on to the potion I made with Gwyn. It's potentially the only way to find her.

I take it out from where I hid it, grab my spell book, and flip through. I remember seeing something in here that uses blood and tracking.

As I'm searching, I come across something interesting. I tuck it into the back of mind. I'm not sure why but it seems important.

When I find what I'm looking for, I sag in relief. Luckily, the few drops that she added to the potion originally will suffice. I pour the potion into my rune-covered bowl, swirling it around a few times, carefully not to spill any. I close my eyes and take a deep breath. I pour my color magic into the bowl. It swirls with the liquid, and when I open my eyes I gasp. The reawakened potion gives me a brief glimpse of Gwyn.

She's in a white, almost clinical-looking room in a fucking *cage*. Just like the witches we saw the last time. I growl and the image disappears. Fuck. It's too bad I wasn't able to see who's behind all this. Although, I'm fairly certain I already know. That woman who's been hanging around here. The one who was spying on Gwyn and me while we were making this very potion.

It's fine, I remind myself. I'm going to find her soon and figure out who's responsible. And then they will *pay*.

I pour more magic into the potion and speak the incantation I need.

"The blood that spilled
Will reveal the path.
Or thy responsible
Shall face my wrath.

Maiden free me.
Mother bolster me.
Crone guide me.
So mote it be."

I feel the Three-Faced Goddess wrap around me and let her calm me just the slightest as I feel a tug in my gut. I know where she is.

Now that I'm able to go to her, I don't feel quite as crazed as when I was driving to the shop. Don't get me wrong, I'm still brimming with nervous rage, but knowing that I'm on my way to her calms me just enough. Although, when I come across that redheaded bitch I'm going to throw down like no other.

It takes me twenty minutes to drive there, and by the time I arrive I'm ready to spill the nonexistent contents of my stomach. The house is in the middle of nowhere, which makes sense considering all the kidnappees. There's nothing remarkable about this house. Honestly, any other time I would pass right by it without thinking anything was amiss. As it is, I can feel the tug in my gut from the spell tighten to a point that I feel like it's about to snap and I know Gwyn is close.

I park my car down the street, ensuring I don't give myself away. I sneak through the trees lining the property, and when I get close enough, I release my color magic, making myself not quite as vis-ible. If anyone looks close enough they'll be able to see something is different, especially when I move, but it's better than nothing.

I take out my phone, realizing that I should attempt to contact the girls, but curse when I realize I don't have any service. Fuck it. I'm not waiting any longer.

I survey the residence, trying to figure out the best plan of attack. Would it be too stupid to go in through the front door? I circle the house to see if there's a better way in. I'm just about to say fuck it and take my chances when I spot a covered staircase that could lead only to a basement. My breaths quicken along with my heart rate, but I sneak toward it, making sure there's no one around. The coast is clear, and when I reach the double doors that look like they were deliberately made to appear inconsequential I hold my breath. Of course there's a lock, but with a small burst of my magic, it opens easily.

As soon as the doors open, the tug intensifies until it's so strong that it's literally pulling me forward.

I'm relieved to see that there are lights on, and when I reach the bottom, I slowly creep forward, sticking to the walls and shadows. My breath whooses out of me as I realize that the only ones in here are the missing witches. And then I spot Gwyn. No force in the world could stop me from rushing to her.

She's in a cage, just like in the vision. All of the witches are unconscious, eight in total including Gwyn, and I wonder if there is some sort of spell on the cages to keep them subdued. The thought both makes me grateful that they don't have to be awake and miserable, but at the same time boils my blood at the fact that they can't fight back, even with words.

This also means that I will have to do all of this on my own. It's not a new concept for me, and I do enjoy proving to everyone what a badass I am, but I've never had to prove it with the stakes this high before.

I kneel down next to Gwyn's cage and examine the lock. It doesn't look complex, but when I push my magic into it, it's instantly repelled and I fall backward onto my ass.

"*Fuck*," I quietly curse. That's some strong magic.

I hold up my hands and this time I touch my finger to the bars, testing it. That gives me no issue, but as soon as I reach in between them, a zap runs through my hand and up my arm and I hiss in a sharp breath. The next time, I rest my hands just over where I can feel the magical barrier. I slowly release a stream of magic to surround it. Then, I *push*. The magic is unlike anything I've ever encountered before. And it feels *off*. It releases an oily black aura that makes me feel dirty. And not the good kind of dirty.

Nothing. I curse and pace in front of the cage, trying to come up with a way to get her out of here. I look around and see that there are more witches here than we thought were missing. Besides Gwyn, there are seven of them. Goosebumps rise on my skin. The same number as we have in our coven.

"What do you think *you're* doing?" a familiar voice croons from behind me.

I whirl and come face-to-face with none other than Vik.

"*You.*"

He gives me a malicious grin. "Me."

He's not even attempting to hide his true intentions or character anymore. There is so much evil in his expression it chills me to the bone. He also looks *old*. Not physically old, but there's a quality about him that seems ancient.

"What is all this shit?" I ask.

He gives me a deprecating look. "I would think it pretty obvious. Do you need help putting it together, Luna?"

"Mother, you are such an asshole. I can see that you're the one that's been kidnapping the witches, but why? What are you gaining from them?"

"Their power, of course."

"You can do magic?"

"Who do you think warded the cages?" he asks, gesturing to Gwyn. He was clearly watching while I was trying to free her.

"Have you drained Gwyn yet?"

Amusement lights his eyes and my stomach sinks, but he shakes his head. "Not yet. I was coming down here to do just that."

I need to keep him talking while I come up with a plan. Luckily, I have a lot of questions. Number one, how dare he?

"Why do you keep them alive after you have what you need from them?"

"I'm unable to kill them and retain their power. I learned that the hard way."

Bile climbs up my throat and I wonder how many witches he's killed in his experiments.

"What *are* you?" I ask as I observe him with new eyes. Males born to witch lines don't actually contain magic. Or at least, they're unable to perform magic. I've never heard of any man being able to wield power.

"I'm a mage. I was born in 1668."

My eyes widen. I have no words. A sense of dread pulses through me—Gran was from that time.

He laughs darkly at my reaction. "I see you're starting to piece things together. Yes, I knew your grandmother. I'm the one who gave her the ability to live for so long. And she threw it back in my face." He sneers in disgust. "Elizabeth and I were in love. I met her through a witch friend of hers, Martha. I was in a relationship with Martha at the time, but there was no resisting Elizabeth." His eyes go glazed as he thinks about Gran and it's strange to see the longing on his face mixed with disgust and betrayal.

I know I should be coming up with a plan to get the women out and escape, but I'm too entranced in his story. I've been wondering what actually happened since Gwyn told us how old my gran actually was. I also have no idea why he's indulging me with this story, but I'm not complaining. Maybe he hasn't been able to tell anyone about it in over 300 years and is taking his moment to shine. Villain monologue and all that.

"The problem was that we were living here in Salem during the witch trials."

I can feel the blood drain from my face.

He nods in confirmation. "That's right. She was accused and made to undergo a sink-or-swim trial. I had to stand there and watch as she was drowned in front of the whole town, screaming at her to go to hell. I was able to keep her alive with just the smallest hint of my magic so I wasn't also discovered until everyone left. When I pulled her out of the water, she was hanging on by a thread. The only thing I could do was to share my longevity spell with her. As mages, we're only able to perform them once in our lives. I had already done it on myself, but I was able to split it between the two of us. It was the only way to save her. And it would also allow us to be together for hundreds of years."

He stops and swallows, pain and anger overtaking his features once more.

"When she woke, she was so angry with me. She said she never wanted to live that long and by saving her life I took that choice from her. She left me. She fucking *left* me. After I saved her life and ensured we'd be able to not only live happily together for longer than anyone could imagine, but I also made it so this would never happen again. She took that gift and threw it back in my face. She said she never wanted to see me or have anything to do with me ever again."

His sneer could curdle dairy and he finally looks at me, his eyes roving over my features, and that same mixture of longing and disgust is apparent. It makes me want to vomit. Out of me and Zara, I know that I look more like my grandmother. It occurs to me then that's probably why he approached me first.

"Then she had to put that fucking protection spell on herself to keep me away. It banished me from Salem. When I learned about you and your sister, I knew that I had finally found my leverage. I sent her a letter, threatening the two of you. It did the trick. She took the protection spell off of herself to keep you safe. She didn't realize that in doing so, it would weaken the spell just enough since it was split between the two of you that I would be able to get close once again. I just wouldn't be able to cause you physical harm. As soon as I made sure your grandmother was no longer a threat and never would be again, I wormed my way into your sister's heart, and eventually her mind with that trance I put on her. As soon as we were physical, I was able to manipulate her. It's too bad the fucking cat got in the way. If we would've had sex I would've had complete control of her. As it was, *she* would still be able to harm you both, even if I wasn't able to. It almost worked too. She was such a good puppet."

"You *motherfucker*," I yell. All this information is too much for me to contain my anger. He killed my gran and put my sister under a trance so he could do the same to us. I was going to be subtle with my attack and my attempts at freeing the witches, but that's out the window now. Which I'm sure was exactly his motivation.

I throw my magic at him with everything I have, hoping to put enough of a blast behind it to set him off-balance. My stomach sinks when he merely bats it away with a wave of his hand, like a fly that's annoying him. I don't let it derail me though. I pummel him with wave after wave of magic. At first, he simply is on the defensive, blocking blow after blow. That is, until I try a different tactic. In the midst of my attacks, I sneak my magic behind him to grab a lamp. While he's dodging my attacks from the front, I slam the lamp into his head from the back, hoping to knock him out.

It shatters and I take the opportunity to hit him with more magic. He's not as quick to deflect this time, and I smile triumphantly when I spot blood both on his head from the lamp, and where my magic sliced him. What I'm not thrilled about is the fact that while he looks dazed, it definitely didn't knock him unconscious. In fact, it seems to have only angered him further.

He snarls at me. "You *bitch*. You'll pay for that."

I brace myself, wrapping my own magic around me, but with all of his stolen power, I'm unfortunately no match for him. He overpowers me within moments. I assume he's going to kill me immediately, but he takes his time torturing me first. He immobilizes my legs so I can't get up or run, but not my arms or hands, as though he believes I'm absolutely no threat to him.

He uses his magic to carve slice after slice into my skin. I'm able to resist making noise for a little while, not wanting to give him the satisfaction, but after a particularly deep slice, I cry out. Malicious delight flares in his eyes and I know that I'm dealing with pure fucking evil. This man is a sadist through and through. Maybe he was once kind, back when my grandmother was in love with him, but it's clear that there is no part of him that's retained any bit of humanity.

I break his stare, not wanting the last thing I see to be his cruel face. Instead, I look over at Gwyn. Her beautiful face is soft in unconsciousness, and as I stare at her, a fierce protectiveness rises within me. I will not let her or any of these other women be used for this sadist's evil plot. I glance down and see blood pooling beneath me. I think it might be just enough for what I have in mind. It was stupid of Vik to harm me in a way that I can use to my advantage. I see clearly the spell I found earlier when I was searching for a way to find Gwyn. It's practically burned into my brain. I took note of it, but told myself that I would only use it as a last resort. I dismissed it because not only does it require so much blood that it would be dangerous, but also because I will be severely weakened from it. I thought that if I was to save everyone, I would need to be at my full strength, but *now* I'm realizing a horrible truth. I'm not making it out of here alive. Vik won't put me in one of those cages like the other witches. He wants revenge against my grandmother and her entire line. He will kill me, and then he'll go after my sister. And I won't be here to do anything about it.

Well, if I'm going to go down, I may as well go down swinging, saving the love of my life. I glance at her again. One last look. My only regret will be not being able to say goodbye to her or Zara. I feel a lone tear slide down my cheek but I steel myself.

Vik makes another slice into my skin, but I welcome it this time. Let more blood flow out of me and strengthen my spell.

I begin murmuring under my breath, too low for Vik to hear, and power my color magic into the blood surrounding me.

Vik chuckles, taunting me. "What are you attempting now? You won't be able to defeat me, whatever it is. I thought you were smarter than this and knew when you were well and truly defeated. It would be so much easier for you to just accept your fate."

I ignore him, chanting faster, pouring everything I have into this spell. It will be the only opportunity I have to save them, and I know it will take every last drop of my strength.

I don't feel anything anymore, not the pain from the cuts across my body, not sadness about the life I'm about to leave, only a deep resounding determination. I don't hear his sick voice encouraging me to give up or even the beat of my own heart. All I can focus on is the spell I'm speaking and the cages surrounding me.

My vision starts blackening around the edges, and I can feel myself fading, but I push through it. Not yet. *Not yet.* My voice cracks, but I speak the last line I need to in order for my spell to be complete. As soon as I see the cages pop open and all the witches regain consciousness, I let myself finally give in to the inevitable. I swear as I pass out, I hear a crash.

FIFTeen

Zara

There he is. My skin crawls at the sight of Vik, even with his back toward us. I knew he was the one responsible for the disappearances as soon as I read Gran's journal. Her story of his deception and thirst for power, not to mention his hate for witches, all made it abundantly clear. Thank the Three-Faced Goddess I've been to his house before. Although, he never did let me see the basement. Now I know why.

I quickly look for anything nearby to use. Ah, there. I notice a karambit resting on the counter in the distance. I flick my wrist, summoning the knife to head directly toward Viktor's throat. He turns to see, and in the blink of an eye, the knife crashes to the floor. But, no sign of Viktor.

"Where the hell did he go?" Morgan asks.

The witches from the cages pause, trying to make sense of what they just witnessed. The coven and I exchange glances before I search the room for any sign of him. What I do find is something that rips my heart out my chest. Luna.

I swear my soul leaves my body the minute I see she's passed out on the floor, surrounded in her own blood. I race over to her, tears flooding my eyes. I kneel down and grab ahold of her arms. "Luna, you okay?" No response. I wipe away my tears before I take her hand in mine and squeeze it. "Luna, please wake up. I can't lose you." My head falls when I feel a hand at my shoulder.

"You brought this for a reason, remember?" Nora says as she hands me one of the healing potions we brought with us.

I nod and take it from her. "Thank you, Nora." Fortunately, I remembered that Luna has always had a secret stash of healing potions in case of emergencies. She's such a badass sister. Always one step ahead. Although I highly doubt she anticipated for her to be one of those emergencies.

I remove the cap with shaky hands and hold the vial to her lips. "Come on. Please work, *please*," I close my eyes and beg aloud.

The sound of Luna coughing forces them open. She looks at me, and I at her. And for the briefest moment, our sister connection is the strongest it's ever been.

"Zar?" she says. "What happen—?" She chokes on her words.

"Don't worry, sis. It's all okay right now." I help her sit up and squeeze her hand. I let another tear drip down my cheek and take a deep breath. "We're all here. And safe, at least in this moment."

She gives a gentle nod before looking around at the rest of the witches in the room. A second later, she asks, "Wait, where is that asshole?"

The girls all gather around us. "We don't know. The fucker somehow just disappeared into thin air," Allegra says.

Gwyn's eyes flicker to me for a moment as if to ask if it's okay if she comforts her instead. I offer a faint smile and watch as she kneels down next to Luna before wrapping her in a warm embrace.

For the first time, I see tough-cookie badass Gwyn cry. "I thought I was gone forever. When he came and took me away, I truly thought I'd never see you again, and it's like my heart was ripped out of my chest."

"I thought the same too," Luna says. The other girls and I step away to offer them more of a private moment.

"Thank you," says one of the captive witches. I recognize her then as the crescent moon witch who came into the shop the same day I met Vik. "We can't thank you enough for rescuing us."

"Yeah, can we help in taking him down?" another asks.

"As much as we appreciate it, ladies, this goes way back, and it's something we need to do on our own," Luna tells them kindly.

They nod before they all look around at each other. "Do any of you have a coven?" Ariadne, the witch with the crescent moon scar, asks.

They all shake their heads.

"I don't either. Honestly, I'm wondering if that's why we got taken in the first place. I think we should form our own."

They look excited at the prospect and we make sure to exchange information with them, not only to let them know what happens with Vik, but it will also be nice to have a sister coven in town.

"So, what do we do now?" Hazel asks.

"Kick Vik's ass is what we do now," Allegra says, lightening the mood for a second.

"Hell yeah," Morgan says. "But how?"

"We can do this," I say. "But first, let's head to the Moon Room and make a plan."

"To the Moon Room," Gwyn shouts. And somehow despite the fear that lives within me, knowing the coven sisters and I are stronger together, I feel ready. No more giving guys power over me. It's time to take it back.

"Shit, there he is. I *see* him!" Gwyn exclaims. "He's in a warehouse off of 34th and Pine."

"What a coward. Of course he's in some fucking warehouse like the serial killer he is," Luna shouts from one of the cauldrons in the Workshop. We're all pumped with adrenaline as we've spent the past three and a half hours hashing out a plan to defeat Viktor. Who knows if it'll be successful, but I'm filled with more hope than ever before.

"Any more herbs to add?" Luna asks me.

I'm about to shake my head when it hits me. "Wait. I think I still have some leftover wolfsbane lying around here somewhere."

"Fuck yes," she replies as I search the shelves for it. "That should do it and then we'll be ready to execute the plan."

"So, where exactly should we be that won't give us away?" Hazel asks.

"Oh, I'm pretty sure there's a hole-in-the-wall café right across the alleyway from it. We could hang out there to at least lure him out."

Morgan puts her hand on her hip. "The real question is...do we want him out of the warehouse or do we need to plan exactly where we want him to be *inside* the warehouse?"

"Oh, good question, Morgan," Luna says. "I think we should definitely take advantage of the fact that he's alone in some sketchy-ass abandoned warehouse. What do you think, Zar?"

I nod. "Totally agree," I say before looking to Allegra. "I hate to ask, but we could really use your charm right now. He uses his sex appeal as a weapon, and I'd love it if he were to get a taste of his own medicine."

"Girl, you know I'm down. Happy to help," she says. "But, I am a little scared of being alone with him."

We all nod in acknowledgment. No one wants to be alone with that insane douchebag. I can't even believe I survived being alone with him several times. A prickle shoots down my spine at the mere thought.

"I got your back, Allegra," Morgan says with a wink.

"Nora, get some crystals ready. We're gonna need them. And Hazel, any ideas?" I ask, trying to finalize the plan. I'm ready to be totally done with this guy. After all the pain he's put me and my family through, it's about damn time someone stops him.

Hazel smirks. "I've got a few ideas in mind."

Luna and I release a sigh simultaneously.

"So, we know where he is and where we're going to start, but how will this end?" Allegra asks.

"As long as we get that motherfucker in chains or tied up some-how, a few sips of this toxic shit"—Luna holds up the vial of potion she's just poured—"and poof, he's gone."

"You sure?" I ask, seeking reassurance.

Luna laughs. "Honestly, I'm not sure. But we won't know unless we try. I think your wolfsbane addition is going to help us out." She winks at me, and I instantly feel gratitude wash over me to have her as my sister.

"Only one way to find out," I say.

We split ourselves up into a few different vehicles and try to park discreetly around the warehouse. We meet at a café across the street, ready to start the plan.

"You sure you can do this?" Allegra asks Morgan. "Not that I doubt you in the slightest... I'm just freaking out a little."

Morgan gives her a reassuring nod. "Just trust me, sit still, and I think it's going to go smoothly."

I watch Allegra's face soften a bit as she takes a seat directly in front of Morgan. "Okay, once you're projected, you'll see him briefly and that's when you need to sell it immediately. Do your sexiest shit and get him in the one room as planned. Got it?"

Allegra blows out a breath. "Got it."

A moment later, we witness Allegra speaking in the sexiest voice I've ever heard. Her eyes are closed, back arched, lips parted. *Damn, she looks so sexy.* We can't see Vik, but she obviously can.

"Yes, the astral projection is working!" I say and clap my hands together.

We all watch and listen in awe with our mouths agape as Allegra seduces Viktor. Gwyn uses her vision power to see if she's lured him to where we want him. She gives a nod and we all smile.

"It's time," Luna says. We all nod.

Nora hands us each a charged crystal. I hold mine tightly and whisper a manifestation to myself as the coven sisters and I all quietly make our way into the warehouse.

We see the room Vik is in, the door open with him looking around in a lust-filled haze, confusion marring his features. Allegra is nowhere in his line of sight. Instead, she's behind me.

Once close enough, Hazel motions with her hands while casting her earth magic, and in a few seconds, Viktor's hands and feet are tightly wound in vines. He falls to the ground.

"What the hell?" he shouts.

"Hello, Viktor," I say as I enter the room.

He chuckles maniacally. "Oh, you? You're behind this? Don't you know better than this by now, little miss?"

"Funny thing is, I do know better now." I swallow the lump in my throat and rub the crystal from Nora in my pocket.

I start to feel weak, feeling him using his power to try to manipulate my mind. My body shakes uncontrollably, but I refuse to let him win. Not anymore.

"Oh, we are a little more feisty now, are we?" he taunts.

I don't let him deter me. I take out the potion that Luna made with my herbs and prepare to dump it down his vile throat. As I get close to him, however, he struggles, knocking the vial free of my grasp. I cry out in outrage as it shatters on the ground, the toxic liquid splashing onto the floor and onto Vik's legs. He screams as it burns his flesh, an acrid smoke floating up to me. At least it did *some* damage, but I totally fucked everything up.

I cast my color magic, hoping to weaken him, but my attempt fails. I watch as he closes his eyes, muttering something under his breath. Hazel's vines become untied and rise in the air, disintegrating into tiny leaves before completely vanishing. I'm blasted back by the force of his spell, and I curse. My eyes widen and bile rises in my throat as he steps closer to me.

"That was quite adorable, darling," he says.

"Yup, it's going to be real cute when we kill you," I say with false bravado. Our plan is totally screwed now and I don't know how we're going to defeat him.

He laughs again. "Oh? Well, then, please, be my guest...go ahead and try to kill me," he counters.

"If you insist," I say and give a wink with a smile as my coven sisters make their way into the room. We all form a circle around him, a full moon for the Mother.

We all hurl our magic at him, giving him everything we have. He blocks and deflects blow after blow as if it's nothing more than a nuisance. My heart begins quickening. What if we truly can't defeat him? He could use all of us to become even more powerful and no one will ever be able to beat him.

My sister's hand brushes mine in solidarity and I let it comfort me. I feel stronger with Luna on one side and Hazel on the other. Viktor's eyes shift nervously around at each of us. His eyebrows furrow in anger and he lifts his hands to cast a spell, now ready to fight back.

My head instantly throbs, indicating he's trying to take over my mind. I hear a few grunts and groans from the girls, signaling he's doing it to them too. He's not able to control us like he did when I was under his trance since he hasn't been physical with any of them and his magic has left me, but his influence is still significant.

"We can't let him win, girls," I shout before crying out in pain. My eyes squint, but I stay focused.

Viktor begins to chant, summoning a fire around us. The smoke and fog fill my lungs, and I can feel that this might be the end of us. I toss the thought to the side, trying to figure out a new plan.

"Sorry, girls. Your time is up," Viktor threatens. His hands motion as he casts a spell of destruction—dooming us all.

"Hands together and release your color magic!" Gwyn yells, clearly *seeing* an option for us.

We press our hands together so that all of us are connected. We're doing the same thing we did on the retreat. The spell that we never figured out the purpose of, but that Gwyn *saw* us trying.

"Now," I shout to the girls, and we release our color magic all together. The smoke in the room is so thick, but a dome forms around us. Viktor's spell slams into our shield. It ricochets off of it and slams back into him. He starts to yell, but then falls to the floor, completely silent.

Before one of us can take another breath, his body bursts into flames. The room heats from the smoke and the sound of metal clangs on the floor. I cough as the putrid smell from his burning body stings my nostrils.

Seconds later, the dome disappears and all the fog and smoke follows suit. The air is clear and the atmosphere calm. The girls and I release our hands and look around at each other.

We all run into each other's arms, forming a big huddle hug. Tears stream down my face, as I feel both comfort and relief.

"He's finally gone," Luna says, wrapping her arms around me. "I love you."

"I love you," I tell her. We pull away, and I look to all the girls. "I love you all. I couldn't have done any of this without you." I release a long exhale.

"We love you too," Gwyn says.

"Ladies, we're total badasses right now," Allegra says, flipping her hair over her shoulder. We all smile.

"Hell yeah, we are," Morgan agrees.

I look back to Viktor's jewelry and clothes lying on the ground. "He's for sure gone, right?"

Luna, back to her brave and daring self, heads over to where he was before leaning down and picking up one of his rings. "Girl, he literally caught fire in front of us. He's for sure a goner."

"But how? How did we do that?" Nora asks.

Luna grabs the rest of his stuff and tosses it into a trash can nearby before walking back over to us. "I believe it was counter magic. Basically, our powers when all used strongly together can take on the magic of another and redirect it back to him."

"Whoa, that's so cool," Hazel says. "So glad it worked."

"Yeah, definitely. I really think that's the beauty of the magic of our Coven of the Crescent Moon," I say.

We all thank the moon and the Three-Faced Goddess in unison and soak up the peace that follows. The silence is broken when Gwyn looks around the empty warehouse room and says, "You bitches ready to get the fuck outta here or what?"

"Yes, babe. Let's go," Luna says, grabbing Gwyn's hand with one of hers and mine with the other. The rest of the coven sisters join us in holding hands.

"How about we get something to eat before we head to the Moon Room? I'm starving," Morgan says.

"Ugh, me too," Nora says.

My phone starts to vibrate and I pull it out to see Joey's name.

"Hey, everything okay?" he asks.

"Yes, everything is fine. The girls and I are all safe. In fact, I think all the witches in Salem are safe right now. We did it, Joey boo. We did it," I say, feeling so proud.

"I knew you all would. Especially you, Zar. You've always been so much stronger than you've given yourself credit for."

I smile. "Means a lot to hear," I say before adding, "Well, the girls and I are going to grab some grub before heading back to the Moon Room."

"No need," he says. "I'm already here waiting and pizza is on the way."

"You're the best. See you soon," I tell him. We end the call, and I tell the girls, "Joey's at the shop and he's ordered pizza!"

I reach for Luna's and Nora's hands again. I smile to myself and think about how great it is to finally have someone in my life who believes in me. Well, someone other than Luna. But most importantly, I finally believe in myself.

sixteen

Luna

"I think I've had enough adventure for one night," I say as Zara and I hop into the car and start the drive to the shop.

"That makes seven of us," she replies, looking around at all the girls getting into their own cars.

It was a crazy night, but we somehow emerged not only victorious, but unscathed. It's definitely cause for celebration.

"I think tomorrow we need to have one of our classic sister days. We can turn on *Practical Magic* and *Hocus Pocus* and drink our favorite wine," I say, wanting to bond with my sister more than anything. It feels like forever since we've not only had time to relax, but also time for just the two of us.

"Maiden, *yes.* That literally sounds perfect."

With the threat of Viktor completely eradicated, I feel as though I'm *finally* able to relax. The witches in the community have returned home, my sister is no longer under a trance, and Vik is dead, courtesy of his own fucking hands. Not to mention that this whole experience has not only brought our coven closer together, but we've all become stronger individually too. We've learned more about our powers and how to enhance them. We should be proud of all we've accomplished.

After we have our celebration, we hug everyone and head home. We're all exhausted and are ready to have no more drama. At least none that's life-threatening.

We pull up to the house and when we step inside, I swear it's as though the house sighs in relief, like it knows that Viktor is gone and we're safe. I wonder then how much of my gran's energy has become embedded into this house. As much as that should freak me out, I find it extremely comforting. I didn't get to spend nearly enough time with her, and even though she's no longer alive, it feels as though she's still here with us.

Binxi greets us, and by us I mean Zara. We each change into our coziest pajamas, and I give my sister a big hug before we head off to our own rooms. Neither of us have the energy for more than that at the moment.

The next day, we both sleep in, and when we finally emerge, I make a full pot of coffee while Zara makes us breakfast. It feels incredible to just be able to relax with her. Even before all the Vik stuff and our fight, there's honestly been so much going on since we moved here. We haven't had the opportunity to just enjoy each other's company.

We watch *Practical Magic* first during the day, saving our classic go-to for later.

After a day of relaxing, we get ready for our perfect night. We put on facial masks, and I pour the wine while she starts *Hocus Pocus*. We cuddle up on the couch together under the same blanket, our favorite fall candle burning and a fire going. It's literally the perfect resolution to all the shit that's gone down between the two of us.

"Lu, I just want to say, thanks for being my sister. I know I don't always make the smartest decisions, but I'm really trying to get better about that. But if it wasn't for you, I have no idea what I would do. I appreciate you always being there for me, no matter what."

I feel tears prick behind my eyes. "I'm forever in your corner, Zar. I love you. And thanks for always putting up with my bitchy ass."

What can I say? Being sentimental makes me uncomfortable.

She laughs, knowing exactly what I'm doing. She takes pity on me and drops the subject. We watch the movie, quoting our favorite parts and making fun of the cheesy ones.

Zara's phone chimes next to her and she picks it up, smiling like her heart is about to fly right out of her chest.

"Joey?" I guess.

She blushes but nods. "He wants to come over. Should I tell him not tonight?"

I shake my head. "Just tell him to wait until the movie is over. I'll invite Gwyn too and we can have a little couples' night *after* our sisters' night."

She beams, excited that we're on the same page. We laugh and talk through the movie, and it doesn't surprise me in the least when Zara cries at the end. No matter how many times we watch this movie and how cheesy I think it is, she always cries when Binx dies. This time, however, she cuddles Binxi close to her chest.

"It's okay, Zar. Binxi isn't going anywhere."

She sniffles. "I know."

She looks like she's about to say more when there's a knock at the door.

"Well, I guess they're close enough to the end of the movie that they won't get in too much trouble," I say. Gwyn and or Joey are early, but I can't say I blame them. It's been an intense week and the need to connect is strong.

The two of us get off the couch and head toward the entryway. One of us could easily answer the door, but we both get it, wanting to see our partners.

I turn the handle and the visitor on the other side is not who we were expecting. I instantly recognize the woman's red hair and green eyes. It's the woman Zara saw and I chased out of our shop. The one who we originally thought was kidnapping the other witches.

I'm about to shout and reach for my color magic, but the red-headed witch is too fast. Her orange magic rushes forward, immobilizing us as soon as it touches our skin. A sinister smile lights her face making dread spear through my gut. What the fuck now? We just took care of one evil mofo, now we have to deal with another? I swear if this bitch kills us, I'm going to be super pissed. I'll definitely haunt her ass for sure.

"Aren't you going to invite me in?" she asks, a creepy giggle escaping her mouth. With a flick of her hand, we're moved backward and out of the entryway. She sits us down on the couch and stands before us. "I'm sure you have questions, so I will allow you access to your mouths, but nothing else. I'm kind like that. Now, ask away before I kill you."

"Who are you?" I immediately take advantage of her offer.

"My name is Martha. I was friends with your grandmother a *very* long time ago."

I groan. I loved our gran, but *Crone* did she lay a lot of shit at our feet.

"How long ago?" Zara asks.

"Sixteen ninety-three was the last time I saw her. The day her betrayal almost cost me my life."

My eyebrows fly up in surprise. "How are you still alive? I know Gran and Viktor had a longevity spell on them, but I thought they were the only ones."

"I'm not old like they were. I'm a time witch."

Zara sucks in a sharp breath next to me. Time witches are *extremely* rare. "So you're from the past?"

Martha nods. "I traveled from 1693. The day I almost died I was able to put forth enough magic that I jumped forward far further than I intended. I was hoping I would be able to destroy your grandmother after all the pain and heartache she caused me, but alas, I missed her death by just weeks. That bitch managed to best me even in death."

"What did she do to you?"

"She stole my love from me. Viktor was mine. *Mine.* And as soon as he met her, he wanted nothing to do with me. I knew she had him under some sort of spell. My Vik would *never* have left me willingly. So I accused her of witchcraft. The sink-or-swim trial ensued, and she was supposed to die. Instead, because of her hold over Viktor, he saved her and gave her a gift she didn't deserve. I watched as she threw that gift back in his face and told him to never come near her again. Days later, I underwent my own trial. As they lit the pyre, I disappeared. It was disorienting at first, but I managed to find my love again. I've been following him, and by extension *you.*" She points her finger at Zara and sneers. "Your blood *still* tainted his mind. And then I saw you *kill* him." She breaks down into sobs then, her face becoming blotchy and flushed. I know this bitch is demented, but I kind of can't help but pity her.

"We didn't kill him. We defended ourselves, and he ended up killing himself in the process!" Zara yells, trying to appeal to this woman, but I know beyond a doubt that she's too far gone. There will be no reasoning with her. I know that.

It's then that I notice movement from the upper shelves. Binxi is creeping along through the shadows, his yellow eyes intent on her. His tail flicks madly, but she has eyes only for us. How crazy is it that I'm putting all my faith in *Chad* to save us at the moment?

"You lie!" Martha shouts, drawing my attention back to her. "I saw it with my own eyes! I saw as he was blasted from this plane. Now I have no one and nothing," she cries. "I have to repay that kindness back to you. You and your grandmother. The Arcana line will end here and now."

Just as she brings up her hands to blast us to high heaven with magic, Binxi lets out an almighty screech and jumps onto her head from above. She screams and attempts to tear him off her, but he doesn't relent. He scratches her face, tearing her up. I feel the moment her control slips and we're released from her magic. I act quickly, binding her in the same way she did to us. She immediately goes still and Zara plucks Binxi off of her head, setting him gently on the floor. He continues hissing at Martha, but seems to realize that we have everything under control now.

"What should we do with her?" I ask Zara. I'm at a loss. I don't want to kill anyone, but this bitch is dangerous.

"You know, I think we need another cat. How about a girlfriend for Binxi?"

Delight lights up my chest. That's perfect. "Get the book," I tell my sister in answer.

Martha starts screaming, panic taking over her expression. "No! Please just kill me! I'd rather be with my love. It would be torture to be stuck here with the likes of you both."

Zara rolls her eyes. "Witch, please."

I sit on my perch overlooking the living room as I watch my humans. They seem so content after the horrid man who always wore black disappeared. It was so annoying not having them pick up on my cues that he was not a good human. I tried to get him to leave by attacking him, but instead of getting rid of him, they just kept *me* away from him. As if *I* was the problem. Why do humans never listen to us animals?

I was relieved to finally have the recognition I deserve after also saving them from the crazy redhaired human. I still have no clue what they did with her. They took her into another room, and when they returned it was with a female tabby cat. Her name is Crookshanks, but they call her Crookie.

I did not like her at first, but I'm coming around to her. She's a bitch, but at least I have a female cat around the house to socialize with. The humans keep calling her my girlfriend, and I don't know what that means, but I don't think it's what she actually is. She doesn't seem to like me either. She's taken over my spots and hisses at me whenever I attempt to get her out of them. She's let me inside her only once, and she was extremely unpleasant afterward.

It's one of those awful nights where my humans invite all of their friends over. It's loud and obnoxious, and I fight between wanting to hide in one of my spots, or join the party to get some pets from the ladies. I don't like being touched by the males, but I'll let the females touch me all night long. In my indecision, I'm above, watching the commotion below.

"All right everyone, listen up," my human Luna calls out, getting the group's attention. "This is the first time we've all been together since the defeat of Vik and Martha. I think it's past time we celebrate."

"Yeah, it's only been a month," the dark one named Gwyn says.

"Hey, leave me alone, I had to go out of town," the one named Allegra pipes in.

Luna wraps her arms around her and pats her back with her paws. "We couldn't have celebrated without you."

"Yeah, you're the reason we were able to lure Vik. We couldn't have defeated him without you and we're not going to celebrate without you either," the one named Morgan adds.

My favorite human, Zara, finally chimes in, raising her cup into the air. I don't understand why, but the others follow suit. "To the Coven of the Crescent Moon. May we always kick ass and take names!"

"What about us?" her mate says next to her, gesturing to him and his brother.

"You're included in that sentiment. Even if you're not *officially* part of the coven," Luna teases.

"Yeah. Your last name grants you some sway," Zara adds.

"How very kind of you," Joey says, leaning forward to kiss her. I cringe. I hate watching the humans do that. I'm not sure why. At least he's better than the dark one. The one I attacked.

"So, what now?" Nora asks.

"Aren't we supposed to live happily ever after or some shit?" Luna asks.

"You're so romantic," Gwyn teases, taking her turn to gross me out and kiss my human.

"To living happily ever after or some shit!" Hazel announces, holding her cup up again.

The group echoes her, clinking their glasses again and making me wince at the volume. I hiss before turning and hiding in my spot, cuddling up next to Crookie. She gives me a nasty look, but allows me to do so. I lay my head down and revel in the peace that's overtaken our humans' lives. I know they're happy and that's all a pet could ever want.

Authors' Note

Thank you all so much for reading! We had a blast writing this one. Mandy and LJ both have a huge love of all things spooky, fall, and Halloweeny. It was a no-brainer that we write a witchy novel. LJ would like to let everyone know that she despises country music and does not condone listening to it.

If you enjoyed reading, we'd love for you to check out other stories by us and sign up for our newsletters! Both can be found on our websites.

With all our magical and bitchy love

xx

acknowledgements

Soooo...this was our first time cowriting. It was a magical (and oftentimes, hilarious!) adventure, but it was more than just the two of us — we had a good crew behind us.

To Iris, our Word Count Tracker Ho. You were there for every minute of this book, giving feedback, motivating us, and getting us pumped with your general excitement. We love you, bitch!

To our fellow Llama Ladies, Tracey Barksi and C.H. Lyn. The four of us are the most amazing group of friends and authors a girl could hope for. We love that we're always in each others' corners, which is evident by the contributions you both added to this story. Tracey, thank you for our amazing and beautiful cover. We're obsessed!

Shiny, formatting this book with you was such a blast and it turned out exactly as we pictured it.

You both literally brought our visions to life, and we are incredibly grateful.

To our friends and family who support us in our dreams. We couldn't do it without all of you. If we listed all of you, we'd be cowriting a whole new book. But please know, we're forever grateful for your love and support.

Finally, to you, dear reader. Thank you for taking a chance on our story. We hope you loved this book as much as we loved writing it.

ABOUT THE AUTHORS

L.J. Burkhart and Mandy Maree live in Colorado where they write and work. Maree chases around two beautiful children, and Burkhart has her hands full with a furry kid of her own. Both women are girl's girls (aka hoes before bros), dedicated to building their community and promoting the work of indie authors. For more (spicy) works by L.J. Burkhart head to ljburkhart.com. For more sweet romance by Mandy Maree check out authormandym aree.com.

ALSO BY

<u>L.J. Burkhart</u>

The Fire Series
Realm of Queridian
Of Love and Time

<u>Mandy Maree</u>

Meet the Teacher